JENNY TRAPDOOR

BY

NEAL ASHER

First published in 2023.
This edition published by Neal Asher on
Amazon Kindle.
Copyright © Neal Asher.

The right of Neal Asher to be identified as the
author of this work has been asserted by him in accordance
with the Copyright, Designs and Patents Act 1988.

All rights reserved.

Cover Art by Vincent Sammy 2023.
karbonkay.wordpress.com/

JENNY TRAPDOOR

In the beginning Jenny dug her burrows rapidly, energetically, but once she started killing, she took meticulous care. She'd ground and sliced away rock, bagged it in nano-silk, and carted it to a natural cave or a burrow no longer in use. Through clay and earth the work had been easier because body compression, water extraction and injection of nano-silk to firm the walls was all she needed to create a burrow. The nano-silk – so much more than the product of a spider – also ran chameleonware to defeat detectors and hide her activities. Still, all had to be done as quietly and with as little energy expenditure as possible because, as the prador became aware that something was killing them, she did not want to focus their attention on the earth below. But, as the kills mounted, she'd become careless and they'd come close to killing her. And now she had no idea how much time had passed.

  Today, self-resurrected from a deep water-filled cave, she headed for the surface. She did not seek prey just yet, even though ultimately aiming to satisfy gnawing hunger. She moved with broken alacrity through her burrows, as internal diagnostic programs struggled to check her function. Not too bad, as far as she could thus far see, considering what she'd survived. Finally, coming to a pipe leading to the surface, she climbed. Gecko-stick feet and hooked toes digging into the walls. The pipe lay well above the stone, going up through conglomerate layers of sandstone and chalk, to wet clay then earth – the walls held in place by nano-silk, so appearing coated in milky plastic.

At the top she paused, fighting the ever present urge to feed. She *wanted* prey above but, in this case its presence would defeat her purpose in coming here. Reaching out with pedipalps she engaged with the lid. The tech in the lid had no power supply since she'd learned long ago that could be detected. She injected power from her own fusion nodes and laminar storage. Initiated by this new action diagnostics began stuttering numerous error alerts from her body for internal inspection. She shut that down and began downloading data from the sensor array etched into the lid's outer surface. No large life forms and she got no technology readings nearby, so pushed and hinged the lid over, it settling on damped hinges to rest on the dusty ground above. Coming to the surface, she spread her eight legs out around the hole, and studied her surroundings with more powerful senses than those in the lid.

The exit lay in a valley. When she first came here a river had run through and this point had been a shallow ford. She puzzled at its departure and the now dry surroundings. Perhaps this was a result of the highly-destructive battles fought on this world, with a climate shift drying up the river and much of the surrounding countryside? More likely an orbital strike had diverted the river. This had once been a perfect spot lying between the prador shore base over to the west and the mid-island defence installations. Prador had used the ground route during the height of the fighting, since flying made them susceptible to Polity grav detectors and thence orbital railgun strikes. She'd taken twenty-three of them at the ford before they noticed the losses and started travelling the route in large armed groups under chameleonware shields. That they had so hidden themselves indicated they thought the threat from above, so she stopped her predation here before they discovered this ambush point. Later, when they pushed Polity forces away from this world, the installation had been mothballed and only the shore base remained occupied. This burrow exit now being distant from prador activity made it a good place to stay concealed, and ideal for linking into her planetary network. Whether it still was, she would find out soon enough.

She eased her entire body out of the hole, flipped the lid closed with one leg and, still scanning her surroundings, walked delicately but quickly to the edge of the valley. Jenny was a trapdoor spider in so much as she bore the shape of one. Trapdoor spiders, however, did not run off fusion supplemented by alien organics, were not a combination of organics and state-of-the-art dense tech, nor did they have three-sixty vision and other senses ranging through the EMR spectrum. A trapdoor spider's hollow fangs also did not run chain-diamond cutters around their rims capable of boring through prador armour, and generally did not weigh in at eight tonnes or carry enough armament in their bodies to bring down prador assault craft.

Reaching the edge of the valley, she scuttled up a boulder-strewn slope. Here grew gnarled bushes like bristlecone pines and, up at the top, squatted fat trees resembling baobabs. She wove amidst these noting a mixed ground cover of fungal slabs and horsetail growths, and remembered bare ground and charred tree stumps flicking out occasional red buds to indicate life. Time had obviously passed but, not knowing the growth rate of these plants, she could not calculate how long. She had no idea when, half a world away, the prador had detonated the neutron bomb almost on top of her. The details remained vague. She did recollect going down deep, carried by an underground river, and dropping into somnolence and self-repair mode, then nothing till she woke in that flooded cave. Though now functional, a cascade of error reports clouded recall and memory disruption included her internal clock.

Out beyond the trees she came to a rocky ledge, above a cliff a few hundred metres tall. With a good view across the west of the island she found it much changed. The red vegetation of this world had swamped the previously charred landscape. Between that and the distant glitter of the sea, low domed buildings now, rather than occupying just one part of the coast, had spread all the way along it. The prador base had grown. That time had passed concerned her, but she slow-danced her impatience as that ever-present hunger grew more intense. Still, she needed information and she needed to know how long had passed since . . . since she had been different.

'What I want to know,' said Jennifer A. Kelland. 'Is what the hell is it eating?'

'Well, we checked and we haven't got roaches, but you know what old ships are like,' said Gogh from Nacelle One. 'They acquire whole ecologies. I found beetles living in the fusion reactor casing. Must have had lead-lined veins.'

'The fusion reactor does not leak radiation,' she said tersely.

'Just trying to inject a little humour.'

'And I am not amused,' she huffed. She was keeping it all light badinage but her hands felt sweaty and, though she'd heard the expression many times, these last few days had been the first time she'd understood what it felt like to have her skin crawling. Gogh, with his Golem senses, had certainly detected her fear, hence his clumsy attempt at humour. What he couldn't know was how ridiculously deep it had rooted. But this was all so stupid and, considering her past, almost deserved. Or perhaps that feeling that she deserved it arose out of the craziness ricocheting about in her skull, which seemed to be throwing dark insect shadows up at the edges of her perception?

She had first seen it down in one corner of the room. It seemed the sweeper bot had not being doing its job properly, and had heaped detritus and dust in that corner – since bound together with some sort of white mould. Not wanting to touch it, because no telling what that mould might be, quite possibly even some rogue nanites, she'd taken a memory-head screwdriver out of her tool chest and poked at it. Immediately a round lid formed out of that detritus had lifted up and *it* had come out. She'd screamed and jumped back, detaching her gecko stick boots to end up flailing through the air. As she caught hold of a console and pulled back to the floor, the *thing* had gazed at her as if impatient with the disturbance and retreated into its burrow. Gritting her teeth, she'd approached and scraped through the whole mess, only to end up with the *thing* clinging to the screwdriver. She'd yelled and flung the tool away. It bounced off the forward screen and *it* had detached, shooting through the air to hit one wall, to scuttle up it and out of sight amidst power ducts. It seemed more adept in zero gravity than she was.

'Trapdoor spider,' Gogh had informed her, while looking round. 'It probably means we've got an infestation of those vacuum-hardened cockroaches.'

'We need to kill it,' she had said, quite firmly, because she knew if she did not speak that way he would hear the quaver in her voice.

He had grinned at her. 'I thought you would have more fellow feeling for it.'

She grimaced at that. The 'A' of her middle name stood for Ariadne – a name she'd acquired during her rebellious youth – and on her back she still had the colour change tattoo of a spider's web. Back in the day she'd learned a lot about spiders and revelled in describing their grotesque habits to her friends. It had been her thing. However, upon seeing living spiders in a terrarium once, they lost their attraction. Also, having grown up on a world where they were not part of the habitat, she'd never seen one in the wild. The last dregs of her morbid fascination with them was dying quite swiftly, now it seemed she was sharing her workspace with one – with a large hairy one.

'I am going to lose my middle name and I'm going to get rid of that tattoo,' she'd opined.

Gogh had nodded gravely, seemed to consider saying something more then decided perhaps not, and headed away to Engineering.

Jenny had discovered that it rode around on the cleaning bot and established its nest directly after the cleaning cycle. She'd sprayed insecticide and dispatched thumb-sized pest control robots to hunt it down, but they never found it. She'd assumed the insecticide had done for it and that desiccated remains lay in an air duct somewhere. But now the fucking thing was back. She'd just seen it scuttling up the wall to disappear in the tangle of ducts and pipes that *webbed* across the ceiling. Pushing herself from her control chair she drifted over to a cabinet and tried to open it, then had to pause and control her breathing to clear the tight panic in her chest. Finally, hands shaking, she opened it and took out a short rod with slide controls on it. The thing could spray a jet of poison almost with the coherence of a laser beam, and was just one of a variety of pest killer in her growing collection. She would get the fucker, and blow those spider shadows out of the periphery of her perception.

Back in her chair she rested it beside her, took some time to steady her breathing again, wiped sweaty hands on her envirosuit and tried to focus back on the job in hand. She gazed out through the wrap-around chainglass screen of the bridge. Aiming for distraction she considered tasks in hand.

The *Shinkansen* had once been an AI-controlled interstellar passenger liner built before the Polity runcible network had the coverage of now. Decommissioned when the passenger numbers dropped below profitability she'd bought it before it went into the scrap processors in the New Carth system. The U-space drive had been stripped out of its three protruding nacelles and, ever since, they'd sat out there as extra and unneeded mass to haul. Gogh had baulked at her suggestion to have them cut away. He then came up with the idea of installing auxiliary fusion drives in them. The extra kick would give them an advantage over other system haulers here. Crunching the figures she admitted he was right. Problems had come later when the stanchions on which the nacelles were mounted began to develop cracks. It cost a large portion of their wealth strengthening them and now Gogh was installing stress sensors to ensure they would not have to spend any more. And thinking on that, she voice-activated com.

'Gogh, have you finished down there yet? Time is money,' she said.

'Are you okay?' he enquired.

'I'm good.' She patted the poison wand beside her.

'Okay.' He paused for a second then continued, 'Time is also what is required to get things right. If I don't have all these stress sensors in place and system-linked we might end up tearing off this nacelle.'

She smiled to herself. She knew that. He knew she knew that. But they had both assumed their particular roles: she the impatient money-maker and he the slow laconic engineer who patiently explained the difficulties involved in keeping an old ship like this running. However, she also knew that his role involved a deal of bullshit and, waving a hand at the screen laminate said, 'Cams 47 to 58,' to give her a view through exterior cams at the nacelle he was working on.

The thing stood out on its stanchion like a huge cored olive. Spread across twenty or more square metres of its surface the painting had grown: a strange combination of the organic and mechanical that resembled the work of the ancient human artist H R Giger, though a little less disquieting. In vacuum just out from this, Gogh, sans a spacesuit he did not need, operated his spray gun. He was painting again.

Jenny sat back and watched him – she found it relaxing and felt the need for that. She wouldn't catch him in his little lie, as he no doubt expected, just yet. However, he abruptly stopped working, hitched the spray gun to his belt, grabbed hull and fast scuttled to a hatch and inside – a bit like a spider. She shuddered.

'What's the news?' he abruptly asked over com.

She jumped and turned, shadows clawing out of sight around her, checked the walls and ceiling for the spider but saw no sign of it, then finally got a grip on herself.

'I haven't checked in a while,' she replied, frowning and forcing her mind away from what seemed a serious case of arachnophobia, and into dealing with the exigencies of now.

Life was good and all, apart from the stanchion spend, *and the spider*, and running according to their plans. Once she built back up again she would be able to buy another smaller hauler and give over the *Shinkansen* for rental. She could then do small jobs that took her fancy and put down a payment on one of the island villas on the planet below. She gazed off to one side through the screen at the green-swirled earth-like globe they presently sat in orbit around. Half of Tanzor lay in darkness and the one bloom of lights in that was likely the city of Lochannon.

'Look at your feeds,' he said – a tension in his voice that could only be deliberate.

The wave of a hand at the chainglass laminate brought up another screen frame, and she said, 'Feeds,' while again berating herself for not getting fitted with an aug on their last visit to the surface. A series of news frames appeared within the frame she summoned. Checking through the stories revealed little more than talking heads. Annoyed, again because of that lack of an aug, she began running searches to glean new data.

'News on Outlink Station Avalon and prador hostilities,' she said to him.

There had been a lot of talk about the prador for some years and most of it had been speculation – the AIs being rather closemouthed about them. The meeting between the two races had been set up and on the whole people had been optimistic. Contact with their first alien civilization would lead to paradigm changes in the Polity, new technologies would arise and new trade opportunities. And what many saw as a kind of social ennui in human civilisation would be dispelled. They expected good news but, just a few minutes into first contact, the prador became bad news. Avalon Station was gone now and massive nigh-indestructible prador ships on the move. She wouldn't have been too worried, taking the view of many that the hostile alien race had snipped off rather more than it could masticate going up against the huge AI-run Polity, but Outlink Station Avalon had not been that far away in interstellar terms.

'Last stress sensor in place,' said Gogh. 'Have you checked the news?'

She paused. He had only just gone into the nacelle so must have worked with some urgency. Something was up.

'I'm doing it now,' she replied. 'How long till you system-link them?'

'Be just a few minutes, but the diagnostic will take about an hour. However, you can run up on main engines.'

'No reason why not – we wouldn't want to be late now, would we?'

He didn't reply

She grimaced at the feeds, no new information had become available since the last time she looked. The news services were just chewing over the old stuff. Then, abruptly, all the feeds went down. She stared at fizzing frames, wondering what the hell was going on, then the frames flicked back into life with new information: evacuation orders.

'The fuck?' she said, and just like that the spider shadows evaporated.

She began checking through these. The information was general, the specific being delivered to cities, towns, communities and individuals below and in orbit. The planetary AI was organising a massive evacuation to planetary runcibles, but also grabbing ships and shuttles to take people off-world. A flashing light alerted her to a ship jumping in through U-space nearby. She called up imagery and saw a large gravestone-shaped thing bristling with weapons. These were a rare sight but she recognised the Polity warship at once. Checking sensor readings she picked up more and more arrivals – all sorts of Polity war-craft appearing in the system.

'I think the shit just hit the fan,' she said.

'Yes, I know,' Gogh replied.

She had one of those moments of annoyance with him – brief and far between. Being Golem, Gogh had a constant link to the AI net so must have picked up on something concerning.

'Check messages,' he said.

'Messages,' she said to the screen. Hundreds of them appeared arranged in order of arrival, but then one flicked to the top and opened immediately, which messages should not do. She realised then it was an open link through messages. A frame opened to reveal a metallic human face – familiar icon of the planetary AI.

'Submind B234,' it said. 'Jennifer A. Kelland you are to hold station in orbit. Dump your cargo canisters on the vector attached. Ensuing messages in your feed are from shuttles and smaller ships requesting docking instructions. You will take on passengers. I calculate that your ship can take five thousand evacuees.'

'What the fuck is happening?' she asked, really for confirmation only.

'The prador are coming.'

'Okay.' A shiver passed down through her body. This should not be happening. Surely this could not be happening? 'We can run up oxygen generation but water supplies are low for that number and, maybe it escaped your notice, we're a system hauler. We don't have U-space drive.'

'Once you are fully loaded, or when it becomes unfeasible for you to stay in the vicinity, you are to head out-system on the second vector given – to the ice field around Calder. You can load up with ice there.'

'And then what?'

'You will be informed.'

'Look, we're a free trader. By what right are you doing this?'

'The right of might, sadly, which we will be seeing a lot of soon. You're a system trader and, really, you need an actual system of human communities to trade between.'

'Are you sure this is entirely necessary? Or is this just an excuse for AIs to throw their weight around? We've all been expecting some sort of shit like this.'

The head blinked out of existence and the frame expanded showing starlit space. Into this, in streaks of photonic displays raised from the quantum foam, fell five ships. She recognised them as prador instantly. Checking data she saw the feed came from near the gas giant Dourth, and confirmed the big U-space arrivals through ship's sensors. Polity ships also appeared and it was only when she saw a lozenge dreadnought did she think to check on the scale of things. Those prador ships were the size of small moons.

The link blinked out.

Jenny sat there shocked into inertia, but then, realising her mouth was hanging open, closed it with a snap and set to work. The prador were coming. The Polity were moving in military forces and evacuating the civilian population, at least, what they could of it. She knew the logistics would be impossible – you couldn't move up of three billion people through the three planetary runcibles and with the ships available here. Nevertheless, she would do her part. Instead of reading each message sent she just packaged up docking data and replied to all of them with that. As she did this she allowed herself a wry smile. The spider had just become irrelevant – her irrational fear exposed as the liar it had been.

'Gogh,' she said. 'I think it's maybe a good idea to get the other nacelles online.'

'Already heading over there,' he replied.

She checked cams and saw him hurtling across hull outside, crossing another one of his hull paintings. At some point he intended to link them all up. She really hoped to get to see that.

'Good,' she said, adding, 'Get ready for manoeuvring.'

'Cargo dump,' he replied tightly.

'Yes.'

She checked other exterior views of the *Shinkansen*. The ship did in fact resemble an old train though perhaps not the one it had taken its name from – its body square in section with a bullet nose – barring those three erstwhile U-space nacelles at the back of course. Working her console she set the right-hand side cargo ramp doors opening. A frame thrown up into the laminate gave her views inside the holds – one painted like the Sistine Chapel. The vector the AI had given her, she slid across with a gesture into the manoeuvring program, while with her right hand she punched in cargo detach orders. Inside the holds rested numerous cylinders ten metres long and five wide, packed upright to fit tightly between ceiling and floor, and strapped to the walls. The straps detached and wound into their reels in the walls, fixing bolts above and below disengaged. All of this was not unusual, since this was how they had intended to offload the cargo out above the mining colony on one of the gas giant's moons.

'I'll keep everything in hold B6 for now,' she said.

'Food,' Gogh replied.

'Uhuh.'

The other containers were packed with machinery, prefab accommodation and other stuff for the infrastructure of the mining colony. B6 held luxury foods, since the conventional kind could be fabricated on site.

'Manoeuvring,' she warned, and in a glance saw him disappearing through a hatch into another nacelle.

Her hands hovered over the controls just in case, but the dumping proceeded correctly. A punch from the main fusion drive set the ship moving, then side thrusters turned it. Puffs of vapour in the holds set the cylinders on course for vacuum, then thrusters on the other side fired up. Like seeds ejected from a long seed pod the cylinders sped out. As they departed thrusters turned the ship again and another bump from the main engine slowed it. The cylinders would go on a partial sling shot above the world and then out. She wondered if she would ever see them again and, making a rough calculation, found that she would need to get to them within the eighteen years, after that they would fall into the sun.

'I'm on the other sensors now – should be a couple of hours,' Gogh told her.

'For the next nacelle?' She continued working her console – setting the ramp doors closing and making other preparations for the arrival of passengers.

'Yeah.'

'I don't know how long we're going to be here.' She sat back, waving her hands and opening up further screen frames. A shuttle was coming over from and orbital bio-printing facility – zero gravity printing of human organs with bio-inks – a dying industry. She pointed at that message frame and waved it open. 'What do you have for me?'

An ophidapt man peered back at her. 'Got ten workers I'm bringing over. Got your docking instructions.'

'Seems a lot,' she said. 'I thought those places were automated?'

'They were decommissioning it.'

'Okay, you know where to go.'

He nodded and cut the link. Talkative sort.

Jenny now eyed the closing up ramp doors to the holds. Nitrogen, of which they had plenty, would quickly flood the holds once the doors were closed. She turned her attention to ship's atmosphere plants already cracking water for oxygen and fast compressing the hydrogen. The stats weren't good – the air in the holds would not be breathable before that shuttle arrived. She detached the oxygen nose piece from the collar of her envirosuit and plugged it into her nose. A second later she sent the instruction to open the holds to the living quarters of the ship. That would speed up making the hold air breathable but, for a time, the air in the living quarters, the bridge, and elsewhere she might need to be would not be so good. She then set an alert to tell her when the hold air was ready. She would close those doors again. She didn't want all and sundry wandering about in her private space.

'*Lancet Broke* here.' A frame opened to show her an old friend.

'You caught up in this? I thought you were heading out-system?'

'We were,' said the woman Deal Crane. 'But we got all sorts of strange delays and the U-hauler we were to attach to was held here too. Mark me, the fucking AIs knew this was coming.'

'You heading out into the system?'

'No, we're coming to you.'

'Oh yeah.' Jenny noticed the docking request.

'We're smaller than you so we've been told to run evacuations to orbit and to any larger ships that can take them. Then to haul ass when the prador arrive. Gonna be messy here.'

'What do you have for me?' Jenny asked tightly.

'Twelve hundred citizens, with minimal baggage.'

'Okay – you've got your docking assignment.'

A series of similar conversations ensued with other ship owners and pilots. Half an hour later the shuttle from the space station arrived and docked to one of the airlocks sat at the centre of a ramp door – as all the ramp doors had. She had to hold it there for a further twenty minutes until the alert sounded to tell her the air was now breathable throughout the ship. She pulled the breather from her nose and told them they could come in.

And even as a bunch of people clad in light orbital work suits and carting flight bags floated into the capacious hold, the *Lancet Broke* began its approach.

'Hi, I'm Captain Jenny Kelland. I guess I've no need to tell you what's going on – I see most of you are wearing augs. Make yourself as comfortable as you can.'

Already she was getting aug requests for com and to link into the ship's system. She allowed limited access to exterior cams, lists of approaching ships and passenger lists where available. She ignored those wanting to talk directly to her, because over the ensuing hours there would be many of them. She did, however, scan some profiles, and made a decision.

'You're in hold B12,' she announced. 'I see that you're all pretty solid technicians so you can help out. If you head down to B6 there are some cargo canisters down there. You can get a manifest read on the wall screen and I've given access to the tool cabinets in the wall. There's food and other items in those canisters – maybe you can organise distribution through the other holds.' One of them was waving at a cam and pointing demandingly at his aug. She decided to turn the sound on, at least for now.

'Okay, I'm listening,' she said.

'Toilet facilities,' said the man tersely.

Jenny blinked, staring at the screen. Up until now the thought had never occurred to her. She now considered just how much mess five thousand people might make.

'Gogh, you hearing this?' she asked privately, after damping the sound.

'It's something I've been pondering on,' he replied calmly.

'Thank fuck for that.'

He continued, 'You've got a bunch of techs down there and probably more arriving, plenty of tools available, and the hold cleaning system and vacuum drains.' It all sounded so easy as he laid it out. They used a water jet system to clean the holds and, since no one liked to waste water in space, the vacuum system that sucked it away dumped it into a tank to then be run through recycling. Halfway through his explanation she told him to tell them, not her. She listened in as he explained, but kept an eye on the approaching ships and shuttles.

Soon he reached his conclusion, 'You have cutting equipment there. I suggest we confine sanitary arrangements to B7, shift empty cargo canisters in there and set them up to give privacy.'

'It'll be primitive, but it will work,' Jenny interjected. 'You're technicians – you know what to do. I suggest you direct new arrivals to the other holds until it's done, and recruit who might be useful from them.'

'Maybe we could do with one of your command staff down here directing things,' said the terse man. Of course, he had little idea that there were only two command staff aboard this ship – that was something she had instinctively not shared.

'I do have command staff down there, as of now: the ten of you.'

'Okay.' The man nodded, then waved the others after him. Even as they departed the *Lancet Broke* came in to dock.

Three hours passed with ships arriving, docking, and offloading evacuees. Gogh allowed aug link from the boss technician – a man called Droven, which seemed somehow apposite – and gave what assistance he could. After an hour and a half he moved to the third nacelle and continued his stress-sensor work there, while diagnostics were coming up clean from the first. It began to get very crowded in the holds and Jenny winced when she thought about what would happen if they needed to do some heavy manoeuvring. At one point a fight broke out and thereafter Droven recruited some boosted types, including a couple of erstwhile Polity marines, to keep order. She only learned later that someone had taken cutting gear and tried to cut into her private section of the ship. She got up and went back to her cabin, opened a locked cupboard and took out a holstered pulse-gun and strapped it about her waist then, after a moment's thought, took up her laser carbine and spare energy canisters. Polity citizens were the height of human civilization, but she had seen now how quickly that could break down.

As she returned to the bridge she saw a black shape scuttling up one wall. Almost with an audible thump in her head her fear came rushing back. She pointed her carbine at the spider automatically, and pulled the trigger. Nothing happened and the spider shot out of sight again. Jenny broke into a cold sweat as she thought about the damage she could have done had the energy canister been screwed down. She got to her chair and pulled herself down in it, the fabric sticking to her envirosuit, and took some moments to calm herself. She hadn't realised just how stressed she'd become. Next focused on her controls and feeds, she felt quite guilty knowing this was something she would never share with Gogh.

Her telescopes gave no sign of the prador out there as yet, though plenty of Polity warships were cruising in the volume of space around Tanzor. The light from their point of arrival out at the gas giant had yet to reach her anyway. However, during a break between arrivals, when shadows started edging her vision, she hurriedly keyed into the system U-space network to see what she could find. A lot was down – sensors out there obviously overloaded by heavy EMR, but she did finally locate a feed from the mining colony to which they had been due to deliver their cargo. Until this moment, the imagery the AI had shown her had seemed somehow unreal, while loading the evacuees had been all about logistics and, for quite a long period, getting toilets to work. And it seemed that any free time came to be occupied with spider thoughts. Now the reality came crashing down on her.

She had located two cams pointing across the sulphurous landscape of the moon orbiting the gas giant, one of them giving her a view of the gas giant itself rising above the horizon. Both cams delivered the same bad news. Streaks of fire cut through vacuum, explosions were blooming everywhere and a view that had once been of black and starlit space now glowed like a cloudy red sky. Across the face of the gas giant she could see wreckage silhouetted, while debris bombarded the surface to the moon. Spears of smoke cut through the thin air and raised yellow fumaroles at their impact points. She watched as someone in an envirosuit drove in a crawler at full speed, abandoning it still in sight of the cameras then running for the base. Whoever that was, she did not think they would be safer in the base – probably less so because it would be a target.

The next ship out was the *Lancet Broke* again. She gave docking instructions for a hold towards the back of the *Shinkansen*, but Deal Crane got in contact.

'We're not docking,' she said. 'Time to go.'

Before Jenny could query that a submind of the planetary AI broke into com, opening a frame in the laminate screen.

'You will be receiving no more evacuees,' it told her. 'Head out to the ice fields on the attached vector. ECS may intercept you on the way for either transfer of evacuees or to give you a lift out-system.'

'*May* intercept us?'

'Remaining ships are hard pressed,' it replied, then cut the link.

Bringing up images of surrounding space she contemplated the words *remaining ships* in light of what she had seen out at the gas giant. Activity had changed now. Ships like hers were rapidly breaking orbit. Larger vessels coming up from the surface were doing so under heavy acceleration, doubtless to head straight on out. Military shuttles were dropping through atmosphere – hard and fast.

'Gogh – we're out of here,' she said.
'I know it,' he replied. 'Near done with this last nacelle.'
'We'll use supplementary drive when needed.'
'Seems like a plan.'
'Get back up here as fast as you can.'
'Another twenty minutes.'

She wanted to say more to him, but then grimaced and switched over to the PA system in the holds. 'Okay people, buckle down as best you can. Light manoeuvring first, then main engine acceleration.' Through the cams she called up frames from each hold and arrayed them across the bottom of the screen. There she observed people issuing instructions, and the seemingly seismic shift of human bodies propelling themselves to the rear walls of the holds. She input the AI vector and got the thrusters and drive parameters up onscreen, but didn't switch over to automatic, which would have taken them out of orbit too quickly and likely resulted in at least some broken limbs in the holds. Grabbing up her joysticks she feathered thrusters, slowly turning the ship. Soon she had it falling away from the world on the correct course, and fired up the main engine. She felt the drag of it, since she had decided long ago not to have grav compensation in the bridge – she wanted the immediacy of flying the thing. A glance at the feed from the holds made her wince. It seemed some did not have that GM fix of their inner ear, since slews of vomit were cutting through the air.

Then it hit.

The *Shinkansen* jerked with such force that she nearly came out of her chair, and certainly felt the pain of a wrenched back. She looked to the hold cams to see people tumbling through the air. Two cams were blank, however, and a third showed boiling fire and black shapes wriggling in agony. Exterior cam views showed the hole in the ship, wide as a grav car, fire snaking out and dying from lack of oxygen, the struggling shapes taking longer to expire. Turning a telescope she focused in on the nearest of the U-signatures her instruments had picked up. The prador dreadnought was gigantic – bore somewhat of the shape of the creatures themselves, and somewhat of a manta ray. She hit full power, bringing the nacelle engines online too.

'Mother of fuck!' said Gogh.

'Sorry but –'

The impacts this time threw her from her chair and she smashed into a side console and cracked her head. She struggled up, wiped away blood and looked at the screen views. Holes had been punched through all down the length of the ship and were spewing fire and human bodies. She crawled to her chair against drag trying to throw her back into the console, and saw three tails of fire streaking in from the prador ship. It had railed them, and was now finishing the job with missiles. She got to the chair and closed across the safety harness just as the first missile hit in the mid-section. The blast threw her against the straps and subliminally she saw the ship cut in half. The second blast hit the departing rear of the ship, completely fragmenting everything there. She saw the three nacelles peeling away then seeming lit inside by flashbulbs before opening up like flower buds of blue flame. She knew what that meant, but had no way of dealing with it right then. Almost without thought she hit side thrusters, knowing the third missile was bearing down on her, but doubted any side thrusters were working.

As she watched the missile approach, she reached out and picked up the poison wand from where she had stuck it to her chair arm, turned, aimed it, and fired a jet of poison. The jet hit the spider square on where it clung to a nearby console. It jumped into the air, legs flexing then curling in on itself as it died.

'And fuck you,' she said, just a second before light and heat filled her world, then darkness.

'Why attack an evacuation ship?' she had asked from the amniotic tank, an age later.

'Because their objective is not to win a war, but extermination,' the AI monitoring her had replied.

Once she had checked and dispelled the error messages that arose when she tried to make the connection, she saw that she had no network. When she had first come to this world, hurtling into atmosphere in a drop shell and smashing into the ocean with force enough to have turned a human occupant of the shell into soup, she had brought a deal of equipment with her. The shell had sunk rapidly and she had departed it half sunk in ocean mud, burrowed down then headed inland. Only after establishing her first burrow to an underground cave free of water, had she returned for the drop shell and towed it to that cave. Inside the shell were her spares and other equipment. She continued making more burrows and each time she surfaced she had found some secure point to conceal a sensor manifold. This chore she had continued throughout her first kills. The manifolds gave her data on the world, the prador positions, the state of the conflict and from these she had been able to ascertain where next to set up an ambush. She'd even linked into the fragmenting Polity data sphere and got some satellite coverage, but now it was all gone – everything.

In frustration Jenny rattled eight feet against the rock. This was a setback but she wasn't completely without resources. In the dense tech of her body her manufactories, with sufficient energy and materials, could fashion just about anything, including most parts for herself, though there were size limitations. She pondered then on other usable materials and energy sources, and knew she would have to return deep underground. Then, even while turning from the slab, she saw shapes rising from the prador base, and focused on them.

Five of the shapes were prador in armour and that they were so openly using grav indicated the Polity had fully retreated from this world. Seeing them, her hunger stabbed with renewed force. However, the other three shapes gave her pause, because she had no recollection of the prador using anything like them. The spherical objects had easily identifiable weapons ports around their exterior. One had Gatling cannons on each side. Some sort of drone. When had the prador started using drones? She considered her options. In the past she could have easily taken down five prador, but now her systems were unreliable, and these other things were an unknown quantity. Not holding a living creature they could be heavily armoured and as packed with weaponry and power supplies as her. She turned and retreated, heading for the burrow but, even before reaching the trees, an impact on her rear end flipped her up and sent her tumbling.

Damage diagnostics came in almost immediately. The shot had been high penetration and blasted plasma into ten per cent of her rear. Her two back legs began malfunctioning. She understood in an instant, even as trees exploded to splinters around her, that the drones had enough heft to sport railguns and shoot accurately despite the recoil. She turned on her chameleonware and accelerated towards the burrow, throwing out ghostly holograms of herself in every direction. Behind she could see the drones accelerating ahead of the prador who, unusually, seemed content to let them do the fighting.

As she reached the rocky slope down into the valley, light ignited behind her, and a blast wave threw her down. Tactical nuke, and now the trees which had taken however long to recover, were all gone. She tumbled down through rocks and scree, the firestorm spreading above her. Next scrambling across the floor of the valley she noted no shadows around her – the blast had contained a designed EMR component that knocked out her chameleonware. She reached the hatch and flipped it up, only for a rail shot to crack into it, fold it up to hurl it smoking across the other side of the valley. The drones shot overhead through the firestorm, then on thrusters flames descended. Jenny folded her legs and simply dropped, even as the landscape all around turned into rock splinters and blobs of glowing magma, finally crashing down at the bottom in a star junction. Above, a shape blotted out the light and with a brief active scan she saw the drones feeding into the burrow one after the other like bullets going into a magazine. The fuckers were coming after her, which was novel – no prador had ever tried that.

She ducked into a burrow quickly, the spot she had occupied becoming a constant boiling explosion. The drones might kill their pursuit by collapsing the burrows, but she decided to be sure. Raising her second right leg she extended a barrel from the foot and began shooting all around her. Again her diagnostics delivered error reports, but at least the weapon worked. Black beads slammed against the walls, shattering and spewing a nano-silk disruptor. Even as she turned and ran the milky plastic sheen of the burrows began turning to a dull grey and dribbling like threads of drool. Walls started bulging and then collapsing. By the time she reached half a kilometre away, back scan showed her no burrows at all while the decohering nano-silk continued to track her. The effect would spread for two kilometres all around where it started, but by then she was out of it and heading down a pipe through solid rock, then slowing along a burrow leading out under the ocean.

Jenny realised she had just been trying to continue as if her mission here had merely paused for a short time. But the plant growth out there, the expansion of the shore base, the fact that her network was down and finally those drones, told her that things had changed markedly. It could be that the war was now over and one side victorious. It could be either and she had no indication of which. If the prador had won then quite likely every human and AI in the Polity had been exterminated. If the Polity had won they would not have exterminated the prador. She just had no idea of how much time had passed, and that was frustrating. Then, as she continued along her course, she remembered this loss of time not being a first for her.

The AI seemed lacking much in the way of subtlety and sensitivity. Jenny felt that its statement about Gogh illustrated that perfectly. She had babbled about the surprising love she had found for a Golem now she had lost him. It had made monosyllabic comments throughout this and, perhaps in some deluded attempt to offer comfort, or merely to shut her up, it had said, 'He would only have suffered through choice. Pain is an option for Golem.'

There was something very odd about the AI, very odd about the situation she'd found herself in. It had blithely opened access to data for her and she'd screamed at the input until it killed her pain, almost as an afterthought. A moment of blankness occurred and, when she came out of it, pain and what now seemed an inappropriate grief had receded almost to irrelevance. Her mind woke to her surroundings with an almost predatory attention. She realised the AI had auged her, removed a neural pain shunt and opened access to data feeds in her immediate surroundings. But what it had done thereafter to put her into this new condition was not so clear. It took her a while to accustom herself to the aug, having to find her way through without guidance and run its operating instructions as a feed into her mind. Something odd about that too, because as far as she understood it you couldn't do that – educational loading wasn't quite that good yet. Once she got a handle on it she was able to look around. A lot of the data just defeated her understanding, and it took her some while before she obtained clear images her human brain could accept from surrounding sensors. She looked at herself or, rather, at what remained of her.

The amniotic tank was definitely not a standard design. It seemed to be a bag of some transparent polymer strung out in a restricted space with protrusions from it extending like threads to attach to the walls, also all the pipes and wires that entered her extending there too. The way she hung in the thing reminded her of a spider's prey, discarded and sucked dry. She said as much to the AI, also adding that the technology keeping her alive did not look like the standard Polity stuff. It had not replied in any verbal way, but she seemed to sense some vast crazy amusement in the system around her.

Little remained of her body. Her limbs were gone and the remainder had been opened out to be piped and threaded on tangled metal that looked burned and half melted in places. The only reason she recognised these remains as human was the human skull, lightly skinned with flesh, twitching and turning when she proceeded from one cam view to another. The eye sockets contained no eyes – but something yellow and crystalline sat in them and, when she made the effort, she could look at her surroundings through them. She did not do this often because their spectrum extended along most if not all of EMR. She did not quite know how to interpret their data and, when it seemed the more predatory part of her did, that made her pull back.

Confusion reigned as she got to grips with all this. As far as she could understand it the AI must have tweaked her mind, bringing out some baser part of humanity to overcome her trauma. She did not like it but understood that denying it would let the pain back in and, so, she began to accept it, incorporate it. How long this took she had no idea – and it never occurred to her to start asking questions until she'd established some sense of self and her surroundings.

'What happened at Tanzor?' she asked.

'The prador,' the AI replied.

'Yes, I know that,' she said with a flash of uncharacteristic anger. 'But what happened to the people there, the Polity forces, how did you manage to rescue me?'

'The prador came. They destroyed eighty per cent of the Polity forces, the remainder pulling out and taking what evacuees they could. The world thereafter has been their plaything and a testing ground for biological weapons. Some humans still survive there – now hunted for sport.'

Her mind now functioning with a snappy exactitude it had not had before, two things occurred to her: the AI referred to 'the Polity' as if at a remove from it, and the events it had described must have taken some time. . .'

'How long as it been . . . how long has it been since the *Shinkansen* was destroyed?' She waited for an answer, but it seemed her question had just fallen into blank darkness. She shouted into the darkness, railed at it, but received no response. Maybe she went a little crazy for a time, but then came the decision to find out as much as she could despite the AI, and she began to hunt.

Jenny pushed out into the system the AI had allowed her, whilst also opening up processing and programs in her aug. She soon understood that the aug and the surrounding system bled into each other, just as she understood that the 'system' as such, was a portion of the AI's mind it had allotted to her. At first it seemed she was limited to the volume her amniotic bag hung in and could reach no further than the walls. She explored all of that in minute detail. The technology, though in an unfamiliar format, was certainly Polity, and this she confirmed simply by the universal bayonet power sockets in the walls. The auto surgeon, folded up over by one wall, looked incredibly strange but, mentally peeling away the additions, she could see a standard auto surgeon underneath. Other facts impinged. She was in zero gravity so it seemed highly likely aboard a ship or space station. Beyond that, she got no further. She needed to know what lay outside this room.

Now she returned to those strange yellow crystalline eyes in her skull. She started using them properly now and felt a fierce joy in doing so. Certainly, they received or deployed and received X-rays and terahertz radiations. She understood enough to know that they could not simply be receivers of EMR because what she now began to see required active scanning. As she began to understand them, and see into the surrounding walls and beyond, she cycled back to the few cams in the room. The AI had limited them to perception a standard human being could understand, because like so much here they were as non-standard as her eyes. Delving into programming languages and what seemed almost an AI facility with them, she found out how to take away the limitations. Now, her perception expanded, she confirmed Polity technology around her, but highly altered and enhanced. She could peer into the auto-surgeon and there see seemingly organic structural changes, a venous system packed with nanomachines, and something sitting inside a crystal sphere that seemed spookily like a human brain. But she dismissed that as highly unlikely.

Her perception extended now through walls filled with similarly organic technology out into a truncated section of corridor. Whatever this place was, it had been altered structurally in a huge way. Perhaps it had been heavily damaged and was now held together with makeshift repairs? No, she doubted that, too, because the level of the technology weaving through everything did not seem in any way, makeshift. But still, she had no idea of her location. She returned to the cam system and to that portion of the AI mind she seemed to occupy. All the while she had been looking around she had felt it around her – data and thought shifting by as if she were a mere human swimmer in a sea and they vast cargo ships motoring by. She felt this to be more than a mere analogue of her mental surroundings, sensing that if she made a wrong move and got in the way of one of those things, the propellers would obliterate her. And yet, on another level, she felt herself stalking the thing, hunting it. She began tentatively pushing, while trying to confine herself to the cam system. As if something had been resisting her just for the fun of it, then grown bored, she broke through.

Cams started to become available to her beyond her room. In the section of corridor she got a clearer view of what it contained, and immediately saw the ECS decal on a door further along, but still this did not tell her whether she was aboard a ship or space station. She pushed out and out seeing internal structures massively rearranged. She recognised corridors and rooms detached, severed, shifted to odd angles to each other. In overall perception she began to realise that they were being converted and absorbed into another structure that possessed some logic, but no place at all for human beings. Then she found the bridge and the corpses there – tendrils running from them and in some manner steadily eating them away. From here she managed to reach out, finally attaining exterior sensors. She was aboard some sort of Polity warship, but one of a design she did not recognise. She understood scale and realised it wasn't as big as a dreadnought, but wasn't as small as an attack ship. Troop transport? No – she saw the weapons. Some sort of destroyer, then.

'Correct,' the AI told her.

'What the hell is this?' she asked. 'What are you? What are you doing?' As the questions spilled out she felt ashamed of the one she really wanted to ask and did not ask it: 'What are you going to do with me?'

But the AI disappeared into its own darkness, seemingly breaking apart as it did so. From it she felt disparate emotions: shame, sadness and anger, but also delight and joy. None of these seemed to match up though each seemed in some sense huge. Instinctively she probed after them for answers and at once found herself in a terrifying place. Separate components of a mind lay here, like separate minds, in fact, but they were all bound together by something and in attempting to perceive that, she felt as if her own mind was coming apart. Retreating, like an animal fleeing some immense mulching machine, her wider perception of the AI collapsed down into something a human mind could conceive and describe: a complete and almost artistically perfect madness.

'What the fuck are you?' she said, but of course received no reply.

Jenny explored further. Ship's sensors now rendered data. The ship drifted in interstellar void but, nearby, rolled a rocky planetoid. She soon ascertained that it must be one of those wanderer planetoids that fell endlessly between stars, perhaps blown from some solar system by a supernova. What the ship, what the AI was doing here she had no idea. It didn't seem to be doing anything at all.

Now she hunted through the ship trying to find the physical AI itself. Since she had little conception of how such a warship had been designed, and since the interior was so disrupted, she wasn't sure where to start. She found fusion reactors – five of them stood in a row – and by their varying designs surmised that some of them had not been in this ship before. She began creating a map of the ship in her aug, filling in areas as she explored. While she was doing this she sensed some action, and quickly shifted her perception to its source. She found weapons carousels on the move, feeding missiles into a coil gun. Exterior view showed her these things slow launched towards the planetoid. She stayed to watch with an avidity that did not seem right and saw them impacting on the surface, stitching out a line as the planetoid turned. All they did there, however, was raise puffs of icy dust. Back inside she closely examined one of the missiles. Nothing of an explosive nature was recognisable, just great tangles of pipes scattered with nodes, as if the things had been packed with fruit-yielding vines.

She continued her exploration clueless as to what they had been for.

She began to perceive that the growth throughout the vessel combined superconductor, optics and a runaway population of nanomachines. And finally she began to see directionality there – that they centred on something. Once she understood that, it was as if a blank spot in her perception had opened out. A part of the ship became available that she had no seen before. She shifted in cam by cam, seeing all the growth now centred on an oblate chamber of ceramal, braced by composite structures like bird bones, and certainly part of the original vessel. And then she slipped inside it.

In this chamber she recognised the remains of the paraphernalia that surrounded an AI. Retracted into the ceiling and floor were the connectors – mushrooms of metal – between which a crystal format AI would sit. Now, at the centre of this chamber, resided something completely different. It connected to the surrounding walls with silver threads and wires, some braided and as thick as a human arm, some as thin as hairs and others thinner still, almost invisible. Here at the centre hung a crystalline growth. In it she recognised clear fragments, etched through with quantum processing grids and shear planes of liquid sapphire, of an original crystal AI. But these seemed to be the seeds from which the thing here now had germinated. Black crystal had sprouted in spikes extending out in every direction. The whole mass was reminiscent of the sea urchins that grazed on coral reefs on Earth, but writ large.

'What the hell are you?' she asked, expecting no reply.

'I am Penny Royal, and I am everything,' it replied, and now she could truly feel it all around her, its immensity and its madness, the fractured mind mirroring the form before her.

'How long have I been in this ship?' she asked.

'A few solstan years,' it replied.

'But I don't recognise this design of ship. . .'

'You wouldn't, since it is a design built by Room 101, and that factory station did not exist when you died.'

'Died?'

'I found what was left of you frozen and vacuum dried, stuck to a piece of wreckage from your ship. You were a distraction whose intricacies of reconstruction occupied my mind while I returned to sanity.'

'I can't have died. That's not possible!'

'What is death? Did some portion of this thing called life remain to you during your twenty-three years floating in vacuum?'

'It's not possible,' she said again, but without the certainty as she fell away through the system and slammed back into her wrecked body. Despite its claim to sanity the AI was deranged – she sensed that all around her. Its perception of reality was distorted. It must have been one of those in the fight around the world, snaring her up, badly injured, from her ship, but badly damaged itself and losing grip on reality. What it told her simply could not be true!

Deep down in her cave system, now underneath the main continent of this world, Jenny Trapdoor entered the course of an underground river, scuttling along above the flow of water. Stalactites and stalagmites were all around her, glittering with mixture of carbonates, opal, chalcedony, limonite, quartz, amethyst and a variety of sulfides – crystals beautiful to human perception and to her full-spectrum vision transforming into an utterly stunning display. Gradually, as she travelled, the river disappeared, having cut down into rock far below. The cave then debouched into a huge cavern. At one end of this was a pool and she saw at once that the level had dropped – perhaps another indication of the passing of time. Before this had once been a flat floor, but now, what looked like the waste from some giant insectivore's gut, was mounded there. The suits of armour bore the shape of their erstwhile occupants: creatures the size of gravcars resembling the by-blows of crabs and wolf spiders. Mostly these prador were first- and second-children, but amidst them lay one large disc-shaped carapace with grav-motors attached, along with prosthetic claws and mandibles. It had been quite a victory for her to have grabbed a Father-Captain but now, when she thought about it, she could not quite remember the details, just images of fast violent action. She moved closer.

She could still see the twinned holes in each suit of armour where she had bored in with her fangs, injected digestive enzymes into the gibbering and clattering occupant, felt it dying and dissolving, then sucked out the soup. This mixture fed her organic components – was in fact necessary for them – and somewhat of the manufactured ones, though the distinctions of such were blurred. However, looking at the heap, she could see something wrong. When she had dumped these drained remains down here the suits had on the whole been kaki coloured or still stuck on the last setting of their primitive camouflage. Now they were multicoloured and seemed to have lost much of their shape as if melted. She moved right up to the nearest and reached out tentatively, scraping a foot over armour. The coating was hard and now she noticed places where it seemed to have run and set, and where larger crystals had formed in it. Only when she noticed some raised stubs of the stuff sticking up from the floor beside the heap did she understand, and then wonder why it had taken her so long to do so.

Here she saw the same display as in the burrow behind her. Crystalline stalagmite deposits covered the armour. She looked up, tracking drips of water coming down from the ceiling. She focused in close on one of them as it hit an armoured claw and ran down it. Close inspection showed her it depositing micro-crystals and, from that she tried to calculate how long this steady deposition had been going. But there were too many variables. She did not know if the water had been dripping at the same rate or if its saturation had always been the same. This could have taken just a few years, or it could have taken thirty or forty. All irrelevant, really. Her intentions remained the same no matter how much time had passed. Even if, she grimaced internally, the Polity had won the war and the two realms were now at peace. Her mission had a more personal nature: vengeance, and the overwhelming need to feed.

Now extending hook claws from her front feet, she pulled on one of the suits. It came free with a crackling sound and she dragged it clear of the pile. Next extruding blades with chain diamond cutters much the same as those on her fangs, she sliced in through the sides at certain points to sever ejection rods and locks, then hinged over the top of the armour and peered inside.

Just chunks of carapace and papery structures of organs that had not completely dissolved remained of the prador occupant. But there was something here to alleviate her pangs. She scraped these out and fed them past her fangs into the rotating grinders of her secondary mouth. Only when she had scraped out most of the suit did her constant hunger wane a little. She was starving or, rather, her organic component was starving. She felt the desiccated nutrients clogging inside and, still checking the data saw something else was required so, after finishing this first meal, went over to the pool, jabbed her fangs down in it, and sucked up a hundred litres of water. Her organic component seemed to sigh with relief, while internal fusion jumped to a higher level.

Returning to the suit she focused on its mechanism and electronics. She required certain materials and needed to locate them. This did not take much effort because she was already very familiar with how these were made. She levered out a laminar power supply and fed that into her mouth, the grinding and cutting processes in there changing for the exact extraction of her requirements. Dismissing a veritable rain of error reports she observed these elements making their way to storage linked to her internal manufactory. She focused on that and saw it had been working hard ever since she woke up in that water filled cavern, pouring out nanites to deal with the damage from the neutron bomb. Now it had further demand on it, fashioning and repairing those parts of her damaged by the railgun shot. The parts were already oozing through her dense tech in ciliated tubes, or pushed and shifted by nano-threads. By and by movement returned to her back legs and that burned out rear began to fill out again. She opened another suit, and then another, gobbling down superconducting wire, copper brushes, composite actuators and, of course, desiccated remains. During second and third trips to the pool she shit out black turds of waste.

When not feeding she squatted, focused internally. Gradually the host of error reports began to dwindle. Greater clarity began to arrive and she understood now just how messed up she had been during her recent return to the surface. Her hunger and need to get back to her *mission* had overridden the internal depletion and damage. The downside of this was as that clarity increased she saw more and more internal repairs she needed to make. In many areas her internals had raised her to functionality but in emergency mode and the repairs were makeshift. She began correcting these. Finally, after many hours, she was ready to switch over her manufactory to making sensor manifolds.

Jenny loaded the schematic to the factory and it set to work but, even as it did so, she found her hunger gnawing at her pragmatism. She had gleaned enough here to make repairs and start on the manifolds, and her organic component was no less functional than in a fed state. However, she knew that the hunger wasn't all about nutrients – a large component of it arose from the predatory part of her mind and her need to kill.

The first sensory manifold oozed out of the factory along one of those ciliated pipes, which deposited it in the magazine for her missile launcher, which she now noted needed restocking. The thing was the size and shape of the end of a thumb and consisted of a mass of tightly knotted tubes. Once she had ten of these in place she turned her attention to internal weaponry and power. The materials for these she took from already open suits, where they still contained munitions. Then she was ready to head to the surface again. She would begin establishing a new sensory network with these ten manifolds but, more importantly, she would *feed*.

Vacuum outside the ship silvered, cut through with swirls of grey to her human senses, and something wrenched through her entire being. This caused a massive dislocation that spread her consciousness throughout the vessel so briefly she became it. She also fell deeper into Penny Royal and its madness. In passing she understood that the ship had dropped into underspace and was on the move, puzzlingly she found herself gazing upon that continuum without it peeling open her mind. Subsequently falling back into herself she also understood that something about her had changed – it was as if part of that madness had stuck to her, and returned with her.

'Where are we going?' she asked, again expecting no reply.

'To the place where I was born,' it replied.

She didn't really understand. The AI came from a factory station or something?

'Why?'

'What are you, Jenny?' it asked in return, and it seemed some giggling joy lay behind the question.

'I am a human woman,' she said firmly, and it seemed the giggling arose inside her too.

'Really?' It reflected an image back of her hanging in a web of tubes and wires inside that amniotic bag, and now there seemed something odd about her, and she knew it came from the influence of that other, insane mind. She looked closer, and closer still. She saw the patches, joins and amalgamations. And then she saw nano-threads maintaining life in her remaining organics linking all to give it a kind of coherence. Her impression was of the web tattoo that had been on the now missing skin of her back. Trying to grasp what this was she fell into it on levels beyond mere scanning in EMR and felt something sharp, distinct and predatory. It held her mind together with its simple focus, its uncomplicated ferocity.

'What do you want?' it whispered.

Anger swirled up inside as she understood what had been done to her, how she had been bound with something she had killed with a jet of poison, but then that anger segued into a response to horrific images of warfare and exterminations swimming through her mind. Those images were nothing she had known or experienced, but they felt like her own and, intimately at her core, they connected with her loss of her ship and her future, of Gogh, of time and of her body.

'I want payback,' she replied, spider mind further integrating, now indistinguishable from the rest of her.

'And I am going to give you the means for that,' the AI told her.

She utterly accepted that now, but noted how she was being groomed – that an artificial intelligence utterly without morality continued to tamper with her mind – tuning it to a purpose. It didn't matter. Fully conscious and in control, she wanted and accepted what it offered and the manipulation seemed irrelevant.

Further information became available to her over the ensuing days. She saw the progress of the war and of the prador pushing into the Polity with their near indestructible ships. She saw worlds depopulated and some simply destroyed. She saw fleets of swiftly and, apparently, desperately manufactured Polity ships flung against the prador and she divined something of strategy. The Polity AIs had known this was coming and subtly put in a lot of the infrastructure of warfare before the events at Outlink Station Avalon. And they had divined that the prador would make the error they made.

Assured of victory because Polity forces expended huge resources just to destroy one or two of their ships, they had proceeded at a leisurely pace. This strategy – to allow the Polity to spend itself trying to destroy those ships – included a whole lot of arrogance and, in broadcasting seeming desperation, the AIs had reinforced that. Meanwhile, they'd been given time to get that infrastructure into motion. Massive factory stations began to appear and run up to speed. Someone, near the start of the war, had used a runcible as a weapon to destroy a prador ship by gating a moon at it, but the speed that further such runcible weapons appeared negated the impression that this had been a new idea. The war factories began to churn out new ships at appalling production levels and subsequent destruction levels in warfare. These ships sported much more powerful and damaging weapons that had not been swiftly developed at the onset of war, but beforehand. And then, because all the AI had shown her before had been leading up to this, she saw the war drones.

Prior to the war, the AIs had created mobile bodies for practical purposes, usually loading them with a submind – either copies of themselves, or highly edited copies of the same. These drones were usually workmanlike machines fashioned to a single purpose. The only AI drones that did possess a distinct appearance were Golem androids. At the start of the war many drones were made to be fighting machines but, as had always been the way in the development of robotics, a lot was copied from living creatures, since those characteristics had been tested by evolution over billions of years. But now it seemed they were copying from whole cloth. Drones were fashioned in the shapes of numerous predatory creatures from Earth and elsewhere, but often writ huge and certainly loaded to the maximum with armament and other war technology. Even loaded with subminds from static AIs they swiftly developed their own individuality. She saw images of them: scorpions and beetles, ants and sharks, tigers and wolves. This production, informed by battle stats, gradually changed, and generally the drones thereafter were those with more ways of manipulating their environment, which meant those with the most limbs, and on the whole those were in the shape of arthropods like insects, crustaceans and, of course, spiders.

The crash out of U-space felt wrong, and Jenny knew in an instant why, so close did she sit in the embrace of Penny

Royal's crazy mind. Some kind of disruption had forced them out of that continuum, and right into the middle of a battle. Appalling devastation surrounded them across a vast reach of space. She knew that with human perception she would not be able to see more than a fraction of it, but conjoined with Penny Royal she could perceive it all, and understand its detail. A large battle formation of prador ships almost like a spike, rotated as, under conventional drive, it headed for some location. A formation of Polity dreadnoughts cupped that spike and constantly bombarded it. Destroyers much like the one she rode in fell on the prador. They attacked ferociously and died ferociously. Through a wave of sick anger from Penny Royal she got the calculation of destroyers blinking out at a rate of one every three minutes and it taking on average fifteen of them to destroy or simply disable a prador vessel. The whole battle looked like some solar event – space lit up with incandescent gas, molten materials and burning debris. Lasers and particle beams linked all disparate ships into a whole, a web.

Penny Royal moved on, shifting and dodging larger debris, lasering smaller ones to gas. The AI mentally drew away from her then as it began to field queries from other AIs with what she knew to be lies, but her perception of the battle remained. Beyond the Polity battle lines she saw a huge runcible gate, steadily travelling through vacuum with destroyers pouring out of it. Penny Royal focused on this and drew closer to it, tried to do something in the informational plenum, but failed, and abruptly accelerated away as particle beam weapons on the gate fired up and began probing out.

'Not that way,' said the AI, seemingly both amused and angry.

Flying free of spreading debris, the dreadnought accelerated, but three-sixty perception remained. The gate drew closer to the battle and its drives winked out. The flow of destroyers abruptly ceased and ahead of the gate she could see the wall of Polity ships opening a hole. It seemed as if reality took a breath, and then it let it out in a massive exhalation from the gate.

'Connected to another gate now,' said Penny Royal, 'falling into a sun.'

The math flooded her mind and, even though she had changed radically, she could only understand some of it. Even wrapped in hardfields the sun gate had a limited life bathed in fusion flame. This vast energy poured into the thing, poured through U-space to disobey the Einsteinian universe, at this end it exited without buffering, and turned into a particle beam three miles across. The beam flashed into the prador vessels and, with slight shifts of the gate, tracked around. Even though the exotic matter hulls could withstand much of this, the ships could not eject the heat fast enough, and their contents burned. The whole prador formation became a vast fire storm with ships falling out of it, burning and gutted, spewing their insides from various ports. When the beam finally died, and the runcible gate at this end crumpled and shrank down to a ball of tangled matter, glittering with explosions marking its collapse, the remainder of the prador ships went into retreat.

'Costly,' Penny Royal commented, and it seemed to her that was for both sides.

They travelled on, Penny Royal lying to passing dreadnoughts and the static, massive station forts. The dreadnought being a Polity ship after all, the queries were not too deep. A hundred hours of travel under fusion drive ensued – half acceleration and half deceleration, and finally the war factory came into sight. The thing looked like a harmonica eighty miles long, its massive square bays spewing out a continuous stream of ships and other items of warfare, and these streaming into a series of four large runcible space gates. Seeking data in her companion's mind Jenny saw how internal runcibles in the factory drew in material from all across the Polity to constantly convert into these weapons. She saw a spiral of drones swirling up like hornets from a hive. In fact they bore the shapes of such social insects being hornets, wasps, scorpion flies and other iterations, but each the size of two or three gravcars and so packed with technology the destroyer's scanners could barely penetrate them.

    Penny Royal wove a course through them and she could now feel it talking to something else – something that seemed almost as crazy. The AI com was beyond her, but it felt like weaponised giants shifting around each other and testing each other. Some kind of argument was occurring, she felt sure of that, and at one point weapons on the war factory turned on turrets to target the destroyer. A part of Penny Royal's mind moved on to wheedling reason and within the destroyer she felt something shift. She focused there and in the AI's chamber she saw a spike of its crystal detach, be drawn to and through the wall by a silver thread, traversing rapidly through the ship to a coil gun and then fired towards the war factory. As it fell through vacuum, a hatch opened in the factory and two miles of superconductor and optics shot out, terminating in a spider grab that fielded the crystal and wound it in. A long pause ensued with the destroyer just hanging in vacuum. Jenny could feel giggling insane amusement from the AI sitting over strata of anger and resentment. An hour passed, and then an ovoid departed from a stream of attack ships like cuttlefish bones and headed towards them on attached thrusters. Penny Royal accepted it in an open hold, the thing crashing in with such force that Jenny felt the shudder in her remains. Some kind of exchange had been made and she suspected the war factory AI had not got the better of it.

'So what did you get?' she asked, gazing at the ovoid in that hold as snake-form manipulators moved in to strip away the thrusters and then the outer covering.

'Your future,' Penny Royal replied.

She watched as the giant trapdoor spider drone unfolded.

Since she had been attacked almost immediately upon her first visit to the surface in . . . however long, Jenny travelled as far through her burrows as she could from that point. This put her on the far side of the continent from the island, where she had to circumvent old spill from other burrows, pass through further prador mortuaries with occupants coated in calcite and blooming amethysts. Here, venturing upwards, she found many of her surface burrows had collapsed and, in frustrated hunger, had to burrow upwards securing the walls with new nano-silk. She chose the coast now – it wasn't the safest place to do this because of the possibility of detection, but it being the coast it was more likely occupied by prador, and that was now her main concern.

Having cleared away wet clay below an old hatch, desiccating and compressing it into new walls, its water pouring out behind her, she paused to make an assessment of her condition. Her internal repairs and weaponisation had continued as she travelled, and she had fed many times on scraps in those mortuaries, but only to briefly quell the hunger. Her energy levels were close to maximum and her armoury full. The photon-dense punch beams in two of her feet were working again, all her cutters and her fangs were well supplied with reels of chain diamond, internal carousels carried a wide selection of missiles – metallised hydrogen, planar explosive, copper-heads, informational warfare and EM packages. She had hyper-dense slugs for the guns she could protrude from her body. She had particulates for the variety of particle beams she could fire. Of course, much of this had not been standard for the original drone body War Factory Room 101 had delivered. However, she understood while observing the Polity forces here that quite a lot of it did become standard. That had been the exchange Penny Royal had made: weapons technology for the drone. She also suspected that something else of a more sinister nature had been delivered in that crystal. She shrugged thoughts of that away and eagerly reached out to plug into the hatch above.

The readout from the hatch brought immediate disappointment. Above it lay further clay and then above that some kind of low density stone and then readings for technology, which had made the hatch system shut down its probing to avoid detection. Jenny extended a chain diamond cutter and worked around the edge of the thing, slicing through the rim. Halfway round and it began to sag towards her. She paused and then cut across the hatch, pushing herself up against the burrow wall under the section of rim she had not cut. The other half of the hatch continued to sag and then when she had just a few inches of composite to cut through, that broke and it fell, shortly followed by tons of clay. She peered up through the hole to see some sort of grid above and, tentatively probing it, found only a form of composite reinforcing. She shifted over to the other side of the burrow and cut round the other part of the lid, and that too fell away taking wet clay with it, to leave a grid ceiling above.

Climbing higher she sampled the grid and the stone behind it. The grid was a carbon composite while the stuff behind was foamstone. These were very much like Polity construction material, though how similar she did not know because she did not know the chemical composition of those. Anyway, it seemed she had come up underneath a raft foundation. It would probably have seismic detectors in it but, since it had been laid on wet clay, what she had done would hardly register. More prador building. Quite possibly, directly above, were prador dwellings! She started cutting with her forelimbs, while extruding nano-silk from her rear and weaving it into a sheet with her rear limbs. Soon she was dumping cut away detritus into the sheet, folding and extending it into a bag. She cut as quietly as possible and felt sure that would not be detected but, certainly, dropping all the debris down to the bottom of the shaft over however many hours this would take, would be.

In an hour she was three metres up through the stuff and started encountering infrastructure like water pipes, power conduits and optics, and took care when displacing them out of her way. Then, her foot clonked against something hollow to one side. She cleared foamstone and found a curving alloy surface. Boring a very small hole she pushed a hair thin optic through and had a look around. Only when she saw a different kind of light entering a grating further along the metre-wide pipe did she realise she was looking into a prador air duct. It was time to flash-map her surroundings and plan an ambush. Retreat was easy enough, she just had to release her hold on surrounding foamstone and she would drop. First, however, she carted the bag of debris down and deposited it out of the way before returning. There were no other preparations to make. So she did it.

The flash combined a wash of the EMR spectrum – with what bounced back being read by numerous detectors all over her body. She released it and an instant later was collating the data. Mentally she built up a 3D image of what lay around her and above her. The image expanded and kept on expanding until it reached a point where readings were too weak. All around lay a network of prador burrows, chambers and birthing pools filled in between with foamstone. In no direction did she scan an exterior and the volume she mapped extended for miles around her and above. The only difference she did register was in one direction where these same burrows where full of water – the structure having submerged in the sea there. And all throughout were prador, hundreds of prador.

Jenny set to work eagerly. The air duct beside her ran alongside a prador burrow on the other side. Using a new technique now she ran the foamstone through a grinding process, rendering it down to a dust of less than an eighth the volume. She went up and over to the top of the prador burrow where it was lined with harder slabs of wear-resistant stone. Here she slowly and carefully cut a wide circular hatch and, driving hooked grippers into it and drilling through for sensory fibres, she held it in place, quickly depositing nano-silk on one side to form a hinge. Then she waited.

Jenny resisted the temptation to run further flash scans. Her present passive scanning gave her readings for a hundred metres in either direction along the burrow. Detecting movement just a minute into her wait brought a surge of anticipation and she watched intently in that direction. Disappointment ensued as a ship louse scuttled along towards her beside the wall. Watching it, she felt the temptation to grab it anyway, but knew that arose from her humanity, for the spider in her had a reserve of patience beyond her own. Finally, at last, larger movement riveted her attention. She watched as a prador second-child came into view, its armour pale grey and two large semi-circular boxes on its back. Passive scanning gave her no hint of any weapons, which was good – this wouldn't be too noisy and perhaps she could retain this ambush point for a while.

Anticipation grew to a painful intensity as the creature drew closer and when it finally came in below the hatch she hesitated fractionally, hardly believing that now was the time. Then she moved. She dropped the hatch keeping her sensor foot firmly in place on it, grabbed with three forward limbs, hooked claws swiftly finding firm holds on carapace edges and limb sockets. Her rear legs braced she heaved the creature from the floor and up. The snatch was so swift the prador only began clattering in alarm as she pulled the hatch closed. With chain diamond cutters in her feet she quickly sheered away those two boxes and flung them aside. They crashed against foamstone and one fell open spilling tools. Clean armour presented, and she drove down with her fangs, chain diamond cutters whirring up to speed and then screeching as they hit the armour. The prador struggled to get a claw to her, but since she was going in through its back it simply could not reach. In a second she realised something was wrong: her fangs were going in far too slowly and she did not want to give it too much time to broadcast its distress. She slammed down a foot with a punch laser and the spill flash lit her abode up like the sun, spraying out molten armour. It penetrated, but not right inside as with previous victims. She fired it again, targeted just off centre to cut the creature's major ring-shaped ganglion. Steam and boiled flesh fountained out of the hole, and the creature slumped, dead.

In frustrated anger Jenny continued boring with her fangs and finally broke through armour and then through fractured carapace. She immediately injected digestive enzymes and they quickly went to work – fluids boiling out of the punch laser hole. She sucked, drawing in juices and half-dissolved chunks of organ. Her organics reacted – running hot and eager and much faster than they had when she had been scraping out shells below. She felt a surge of pleasure at the intake of fresh nutrients, but it quickly reached a plateau and died. By the time she had finished she felt just as hungry again. Yes, she had taken in some good nutrients, but one aspect of the feeding process had been lacking. Her prey had not suffered. She had not felt it struggling and dying as she fed upon it. And now, of course, she needed to garner information from this victim.

Jenny sealed the hatch all around with silk, collected up the tools and put them back in the open box, and reattached both boxes to the dead prador with silk before dragging the lot down below. She paused in a granite walled side burrow just for a second, but then decided she needed more open space in which to work, so dragged her victim off to the nearest mortuary. The cave was a small one and, when she arrived, she noted that she had been neater and more meticulous here, in the early days, because she had stacked the prador in rows, like plates in a dryer, rather than thrown them into a heap. A clear area lay in the centre with these rows all around up the walls, three prador high, the bottom row being first-children and the top two, second-children. The thought that her mind must have been different during those early hunts arose for her inspection then passed. She turned her attention to her latest victim.

First she pressed a foot down on its armour and ran deep scan and laser spectrographic analysis. The armour lay only a few centimetres thick and was of radically different materials. It did not contain exotic matter additives like their ship armour, as had been her fear, but was laminated with stress-dispersion layers and other 2D meta-materials. She rocked back, puzzled, for it had the characteristics of AI-designed armour for Polity ships and combat suits. This, on top of the foamstone and other construction materials of this place, made her realise the prador had been incorporating Polity tech. No matter. She had to design a solution. She created a model of the armour in her mind and ran chain diamond cutters against it there. She found that some layers acted to clog the diamond cutters, others to blunt them. She began to come up with solutions – enzyme acids for those softer layers, electrostatic disruption of meta-materials, laser cutting in places – and began trying all these out via one of the cutters on a foot. It took some time, as if the armour had actually been designed to defeat the likes of her, but finally she had her solution: tuned down punch laser to heat the point of penetration, then a combination of two enzyme acids to burn in but also act as lubricants for the chain diamonds. This was all very well for a foot cutter, but she would need to redesign her fangs and related systems as they were more complicated. But first, she needed to find out what else she might have to contend with.

Using the methods she had ascertained she cut open the suit, glad to find that the basic mechanism of the thing remained unchanged. Hinging back the top released sulphurous gas and steam and she found a lot of still dissolving remains inside, and sucked them up making a sound like someone with a straw reaching the bottom of the glass. She then stripped out remaining carapace, pulling legs and under-arms out of their covering and discarding them to one side – they still contained meat and she would get to them later. She then used air and water jets to clean the interior until finally it all but gleamed. She found an optic port, plugged in and began to read data. A moment later she flicked on terahertz reception in scanning and felt a surge of anger and just a little trepidation. The suit was broadcasting in that range so that meant its signals were cutting through the ground. She backed off abruptly and did a flash scan and at once detected anomalies. Objects were moving through the burrows back the way she had come, and she suspected more of those drones she had seen earlier were coming after her.

Jenny's immediate instinct, now she was fully functional, was to go after the machines. But her caution overrode that. If this simple second-child possessed such tough armour, those other machines would have the same if not better and be difficult to destroy. Also, she needed more data – ever more data if she was to get back into her routine of feeding. She hurriedly traced out the system in this suit, locate the terahertz emitter and shut it down. A full spectrum scan then picked up emissions in other radiations, and she discovered that emitters were imbedded all over in the armour. She did not have the time to locate and shut them down individually, so working frenetically, cutting where she could not separate out what she wanted by other means, she extracted the computer system of the armour, along with its laminar power supply, detaching it from all those emitters. She ended up with a series containers linked together by optics and s-con wires. Emptying one of the tool boxes she put all this inside, attached it to her abdomen with silk, and then headed for the exit. Here she paused and accessed her weaponry. Opening a hatch in her side she folded out a slug thrower and loaded it with metallised hydrogen missiles. Into these she wrote a program from her collection, and slow fired them all around her. The missiles thumped in the walls burying themselves, some bounced out – it didn't matter – and none exploded. Then, as she departed the chamber, she sent a signal to activate their sensors. They ignored her, but other movement would activate them.

Jenny sped through rocky burrows. She wanted a good distance before heading up. This entire section of her network was full of burrows that had collapsed in less dense material like clay, limestone and conglomerate. She also desperately wanted to scan her surroundings but, the moment she used any scanning, she would reveal her location to the pursuers. At least, she thought, they lay behind her. . . She skidded to a halt, instincts screaming. She had no doubt that the prador above now knew precisely what was down here. They didn't have AI, or at least didn't have it when last she hunted them, but they did have computers and excellent methods of information storage and exchange. They had known about her in the past when they tried to kill her with a neutron bomb. Her previous recent reappearance would have alerted them. They also had war machines that could enter these burrows to hunt her down. It would be stupid to assume that they had only come in behind her.

She moved on more slowly, thinking this through, then at the next junction, rather than continue heading inland as had been her instinct, she took a left and headed along the coast. At the next opportunity she took a pipe leading upwards but in that felt a wave of terahertz scan passing through her.

Damn. . .

How far could their scan penetrate? How much data did it render for them? Reluctantly she put on her energy-hungry chameleonware, then moved fast, now heading for the sea. Ahead a clay burrow steadily grew tighter as she traversed it, pushed down into an oval by the weight above. She fired a BIC laser along it, rendering ultra-sound reading. It wouldn't give away her location but would tell her whether the burrow ahead had collapsed. A moment later she found out it had, backed up and turned, heading for a turning she had passed previously. As she moved she picked up a rumbling and slight shuddering all around. The drones had found the chamber were she had taken the remains of her latest victim. Nearby lay the turning she was aiming for – perhaps she could find a way to the sea up there, or perhaps all the burrows along the coast had collapsed. This became a secondary concern when the spherical drone slid into view ahead of her.

Jenny thought she should object, but the thought seemed just an intellectual exercise – her destination being as certain as fate. A further chamber had opened out beside the one in which she hung in her amniotic sac. Penny Royal shifted the spider drone through the interior of the ship like a bolus of food through intestines to finally deposit it there, then set to work on it at once. Silvery tendrils, some hair thin and some braided and thick as a leg, writhed in. These sported manipulators, ranging from those the size of human hands down to those invisible to the human eye, and they steadily disassembled the drone. As the contents came out and spread all around, as if in a slow explosion, it seemed impossible that they had all come from inside that thing.

'Dense tech,' said Penny Royal.

The disassembly continued until the drone no longer had recognisable form. The silvery strands and manipulators moved so fast that in places they blurred. She saw lasers stabbing and heard things crackling. Some components were swept away and disappeared into the walls. Others returned, or perhaps they were the same ones altered elsewhere. Components that remained, even though of solid materials, shifted and changed like hunting amoebas. She tried to get closer to Penny Royal's mind, to understand what it was doing. At once she fell into a vast schematic that seemed to extend to infinity. Fragments of data spilled over. She saw nanotech being even further reduced or redesigned. She saw processes that seemed to extend below the nano even to the redesign of atoms, but that seemed improbable so perhaps somehow the mind was lying to her.

Withdrawing, because the complications rolled beyond her, she wondered why the AI, so radically altering this drone, had not simply built what it wanted from scratch. But she then understood that other motives were here – the delivery of that crystal had been one of them. The AI's mind was a complicated, fractured thing with layers of purpose, some in conflict. It was further beyond her understanding than the schematic of the drone.

    As the drone started to come back together she again tried the schematic and this time began to understand the weapons inside it and the purpose of the fangs it could extrude from its chelicerae. She traced the vague order in there in the same way she had tracked down Penny Royal in this ship, and found an empty space within the thing's body. This, she understood, had been where its mind was to be located, but Room 101 had supplied no mind. She saw then how the compacting and changing had left a larger space there, with a web of channels throughout extending from it. She inspected that space. It was the shape of a human female lying face down with arms extended. The head was tilted up just behind the spider's head, while the body and legs lay in the cephalothorax ahead of the abdomen.

    Acceptance of what that meant came when the strange autosurgeon in here rose up and walked on silvery bird legs and wrapped itself around her amniotic bag. Fluid rapidly drained away, displaced by some gas to keep the bag inflated, then a touch started a decoder in that skin, and it fizzed to dust like fuse paper. The surgeon caught her in numerous limbs and began peeling away the ship wreckage that had been used like bones to support the softer parts of her. She opened out and uncoiled and now she began to see her true shape.

She was a limbless torso and head with a web extending from both, formed of glassy organics. All over that torso and in her skull she recognised data sockets both organic and mechanistic. Able to link to the surgeon and peer through its sensors as well as her own she managed to construct a composite image – a schematic of what she was all the way through. She retained the human organs of that torso to support her brain, but much changed and adapted and with strange meta-materials woven through, while the heart did not pump blood. Holding her, as delicate as a spider's web, or perhaps some grotesque butterfly, the surgeon began to move her towards the drone. In this moment, seeing what sat in the top of her skull, she truly understood that she was the crazy, horrifying project of a shattered, distorted but still vastly intelligent mind, for in the top of her skull, linked into her mind and into its support system too, was the trapdoor spider from her bridge, entire.

Pain wracked her, but it seemed the only recognisable part of weird array of feelings. Her torso and head went into the space made for them, and thousands of connections engaged. The web fed into the spaces for her missing limbs, fixed along structures the surgeon printed there. These, she saw as the work progressed, began to form a full human skeleton. Why? Perhaps some strange complex joke about the human form with a spider in its skull, controlling a larger spider. This being a product of brilliant madness it did not need to make sense to her. From the printed bones the glassy strands of the webs branched into channels, extending throughout, down into the spider limbs, into the fangs, the armament – a nervous system being installed. She choked as a series of tubes went into her mouth, connecting down into her bronchus and oesophagus, but the feeling bled away as her lungs started breathing. She shrieked as plugs engaged into her eye sockets, but only mentally. And the AI shrieked along with her in agonised creative joy and a whole swathe of emotions she could not even recognise. Components interweaved in further complexity buried her, and as the AI closed up the drone around her, her engagement with it continued with unbearable intensity. She felt herself amalgamating, becoming, and as all those strands and machines retreated she was the spider.

'Why?' she managed to ask.

All she got in response was a wave of something, part confusion, part happy shame – another mixture difficult to parse. Then the AI was gone again, and alone she continued to integrate, knowing she was a killer somewhat beyond the products of Room 101 now.

She was, she understood, a product of terrible art.

No reason now for further concealment. Jenny launched a powerful aggressive scan at the drone. Even as it went, and bounced back with its data, she remembered her first explosive comprehension of what she was inside Penny Royal's ship. The AI had packed her with everything – with a redundancy of systems and weapons that had been taken as far as the AI could go with its own form of dense tech. This perception of herself had waned over the years because the traps and the killing were so uncomplicated, and she had no need for everything she was.

The data slammed back into her and for a moment seemed to be sliding from her grip, but then one of those systems booted up, in small black crystals scattered throughout her being. Instead of puzzling over the data she simply incorporated it, and saw the drone for what it was in an instant.

It was loaded with weapons – missile launchers, railguns and particle beamers set in holes through its armour. The armour lay a good ten centimetres thick, laced with super conductor connected to thermocouples that could feed some of the energy of attack back into its laminar storage, or eject it using hyper-compressed nitrogen or through its lasers – it had those too. Its main source of power came from a fusion reactor that topped up laminar storage. It had a grav engine in there, and ion thrusters also sticking through holes in the armour. At the centre the flash-frozen ganglion of a first-child controlled it. She understood the thing as a whole, and addressed its weaknesses, even as it opened fire.

Jenny leapt up, but there wasn't much room to avoid the stab of that particle beam. She raised her forelimbs, almost instinctively bringing online something she had forgotten about. Like a sheet of amber a hardfield flicked into being between her limbs. The beam splashed on it and using superior thermocouples, she ejected the feedback as steam through the rear ones of rows of ports down her body, and shot forwards. Also propelling herself with her legs against the burrow walls, she went supersonic in less than a second, and then slammed into the drone wrapping her legs around it. She had already understood the vulnerability here: the drone's tough armour would take too long to penetrate down here in the burrows, but its weakness lay in those weapons and thrusters – too many holes. Even as she gripped tightly her feet covered many of them. She fired four punch lasers. A railgun distorted even while firing and put a slug off course into the side of a hole. The particle beam flared out, but the armour had sufficient s-con to draw off the heat. She burned in, still looking, and located an internal missile carousel, and hit that with multiple blasts. The missiles – chemical loads wrapped around bars of metalized hydrogen – began exploding. She scrambled over the thing and past, turning to watch. The explosions continued, blowing debris and burning matter out of the ports. Still scanning she saw the ganglion case distort, and then break open, spilling organic detritus and coolant. It was done. She watched a moment longer, expecting it to drop, but it just floated there with the fires guttering and turning to black smoke. It seemed the internal carnage had not taken out the gravmotor.

Jenny moved swiftly on, feeling a wondrous and deep satisfaction with the encounter, then abruptly slammed to a halt when she realised what had changed. Her hunger, a constant madly driving force, had waned. She started moving again, slower now as she inspected herself internally and assessed what had happened with the new processing that had opened out within her. Why now? Why had the redundancies kicked in now? Yes, she had been in great danger facing that drone, but she had been in equal danger when she had gone to the surface. She could only surmise that she had been so damaged then it hadn't been possible for her to bring those other systems online. Now scanning internally she studied what had fired up. Initially she focused on what occupied the human mould within her cephalothorax. As ever, the bloody meat of that, strewn along printed bones, repelled her and she switched her attention out from it.

Extra processing she had forgotten about over the years had brought her greater almost AI level clarity. It lay in those black crystals scattered along her internal web and, she had no doubt, they were of the same substance as the black AI Penny Royal. She brought her attention to them, trying to divine how they had activated, and then noticed something had changed about them. Only by tweaking internal scanning could she properly see the change. Now, instead of being impenetrable black and unknowable, the crystals had cleared. She could now, taking the scan down to the micro and nano-scopic, see quantum grids, sapphire sheer planes, and the quantum effects of single atom processing. What did that mean? She had no idea so turned her attention to other internal activations.

Like much of her system, that of hardfield generation was distributed. She had vague recollection of using the hardfields during her first time here when the fighting between prador and Polity had been at its height. Her use of them had waned as she got into her routine of trapping and feeding, and along with that her memory of them had faded too. Now it had come back hard along with understanding and perception of all her other 'redundancies'. Changes were occurring in them too. A railgun, long just an inert mass within her lying below her human form and tangled with everything else, was clarifying, as below it the magneto-electrostatic tube of a particle weapon began emptying out systems that had come to dwell inside it. On a mental level a whole host of informational warfare programs had become accessible, while her scattered lasers were introducing the tweaks for vortex beams to carry them. It was all so utterly puzzling. It seemed she had climbed into a higher active state. Perhaps the previous damage had taken off some kind of limiter? Even as she thought that, she thought no. This was all something to do with Penny Royal and those crystals clearing. But what, she had no idea.

Back to first principles. She had fed for it seemed the drones down here, hunting her, satisfied a hunger for which the act of killing seemed an integral part. But now the hunger, as ever, was returning. She need think no further than that

Time to hunt those drones.

The integration just seemed to go on and on. Whenever she felt a grasp on some portion of the vast complexities inside her, it slipped away when she found something else. How was she supposed to handle all this? And how, now it had steadily risen inside her, could she feed this terrible, awful hunger?

Movement at least became something she could handle. It felt so strange to be moving on eight limbs after being human and, as she had struggled with this it seemed the spider moved in her skull in consonance. But then, as she began to get full control of it, that feeling faded, almost as if the spider there was dissolving.

She moved around in the limited space of the conjoined chambers. At one point, when she went over to the autosurgeon, it activated and fled to the furthest point away from her. When she went over to it again, instead of fleeing it wrapped itself up in a tight ball and dropped to the floor. She inspected it closely and got confirmation of something she thought she had seen before: a human brain sat inside the autosurgeon, flooded with a support nanofluid. And this further confirmed that Penny Royal enjoyed playing with human beings, and had a penchant for amalgamating them with machines.

'Who are you?' she asked, her voice issuing from a mechanism in her drone body into the highly oxygenated air another mechanism breathed for her.

The surgeon just tightened up even further, so she turned away and crossed the room. The door opened without a problem and she ventured out into the truncated corridor lying beyond. She headed in the direction of the AI's chamber, but after just twenty metres encountered the tangled technological ecology of the ship. Again she mentally reached for Penny Royal, seeking answers, but mostly for some relief from the intensity of input from her drone body. She could walk, breathe, look and now speak. She could peer into the AI realm, but peering into herself seemed too chaotic and complicated for her. She wasn't sure what she did – whether driven by her desperation, operating systems within her, or a response from the AI – but the tangle ahead of her began to open out. She moved into an expanding tube through it, delicately propelling herself ahead in zero gravity with her feet hooking on shifting pipes and meta-material surfaces.

The tube wound on through the ship and, glimpsing into the sensory system when able, she saw it finally terminating against the chamber that contained the AI. A wall peeled open ahead of her – shreds of it lifting and rolling back to finally make an opening wide enough for her. She entered, drifting, then caught hold of floor grids and pulled herself down. The AI had changed since last she had seen it. It seemed more perfectly black and spiky and she could detect no sign of that original crystal. Fewer of those silvery strands connected to it and she felt some sense of centrality here, and the weird draw and twist of U-space manipulation. She got the impression that somehow it was consolidating.

'We approach your destination,' it intoned.

'I cannot handle everything you've loaded in me,' she replied.

'Human minds,' it commented.

That seemed the end of the conversation and she did not know how to ask for more. She stared at the thing, understanding that whether or not she suffered was irrelevant to it. She just had to fit to the twisted purpose for which it had deemed her suitable. Then one of the crystals detached. It drifted out like a missile and began to splinter into shards. These shoaled towards her and circled her, then one came in hard and fast. Her armour, tougher and harder than Polity state-of-the-art, had the resistance of butter to it, and it penetrated deep. She screamed, because in this new body she had not expected pain. The others sped in, slamming inside her as she shot around the chamber trying to avoid them, and trying to bring weapons online. Extra mental processing opening as the crystals connected to her internal web had its own kind of pain too, but even in that she found the control she wanted. She slammed to a halt as final shards punched into her body, and fired up a particle weapon. A devastating beam of sun-hot particulate stabbed at Penny Royal, but U-space twisted and the energy went elsewhere.

'Fuck you!' she yelled, firing vortex lasers loaded with viral warfare, then folded out slug throwers and hammered at the AI with them. Her railgun powered up and she fired that, the recoil slamming her back against a wall. With everything now in her grasp she felt incredibly potent, but then impotent as nothing touched that black shifting star. Something washed through her on many levels of EMR. Informational warfare, communication? No, she realised she could hear the AI's insane laughter. Then something hit her, all through, issuing from those black crystals, and she just folded up inert.

'Some adjustments will be necessary,' the AI opined, as silvery threads began to weave a shell around her. As she felt her consciousness fading, she knew the crystals had not only given her full control over her body, but were a link to Penny Royal too. Of course, the AI wanted to see how its creation performed, while it went about other insane tasks.

With the second drone she tried out her railgun, and the recoil flung her a hundred metres back down a burrow. When she returned the drone lay on the floor, the entry hole the width of an arm, the hole where the slug had exited as plasma gaping a metre wide. Beyond the drone smoke boiled from the burned contents of the drone spread along the burrow walls. She analysed this in respect of railguns she had seen in operation when the Polity had been here fighting, and the effect of one drone railgun shot on her. The thing she had inside her was an order of magnitude more powerful, and she made a note to properly brace herself next time she fired it.

She moved on, now feeling potent as she had felt when first realising her full potential, and before realising that she could not touch the black AI. She also felt thoroughly satisfied – fed – so moved away from where she expected drones to be and decided to take a look at the hardware she had pulled out of that prador's suit. As she examined this she pondered too on Penny Royal. She had been here on this world for a number of Solstan months before Polity forces arrived and were driven away again. In that time, though she had avoided Polity drones and soldiers, she gleaned much information by keying into their data sphere and, of course, she sought out news of the AI that was both her benefactor and her demon. Penny Royal had come to be referred to as a black AI, or rogue AI. It seemed it had continued its experiments in amalgamating humans with machines, but also upgraded to even weirder and more grotesque works. For a time ECS had thought it fighting for the prador, until learning that they were as much subject to its attentions as anyone else. Still, it remained a huge danger and ECS wanted any data they could obtain on the thing. She learned that ECS was sweeping up for intensive examination many of those who had encountered and been transformed by it. For her, with black crystals inside her, that did not seem like a good idea, and she had scotched the idea of apprising the Polity of her presence.

But what now? Why had those crystals lost their opacity? Why were they no longer black? And why were her functions now so easily accessible? Her mentality now gave her perspective: that she had honed down to the simple chore of trapping prador and feeding on them, and forgotten so many of her other functions, she put down to Penny Royal's *adjustment* of her. Had it now adjusted her again? She felt not. It seemed more as if the retreat of that darkness from those crystals signified the retreat of the AI from her. Perhaps it had been captured by ECS or the prador, maybe destroyed? No, even that did not seem right. The thing had been incredibly powerful when it made her – way beyond the technology of the time – and with an AI, unlike organic intelligences, there were no limits to growth. Thinking on all this, she now saw a glimmer of purpose beyond mere hunting and killing – she actually saw a hint of a future.

      The hardware from the prador's suit quickly rendered up its secrets to her expanded perception, and from this she surmised something of how the war had been going. She saw that it no longer contained the remote control system of earlier victims. This had enabled a Father-Captain to keep a prador suit of armour fighting even after its occupant had been killed. There could be only one reason for its removal: penetration. The AIs had learned how to usurp that same control system so it had become far too much of a danger. The continued broadcasting of the suit had telemetry, which tied in. If AIs were seizing control of prador suits a Father-Captain would want to know the precise position and disposition of all his children, or soldiers, because a suit seized by the Polity and loaded with atomics might inconvenient. She also noted programs, getting rather closer to AI than expected, since the prador hated AI. The suit could be keyed to fight independently by its occupant – probably as it died. Now she also began to divine other things. That armour had seemingly been designed to prevent the likes of her penetrating it, indicated other drones had been given this ability. It had probably arisen out of Room 101 and what Penny Royal had given the AI of that war factory. But in the end, none of this told her things she really wanted to know, like how long had passed, and whether or not the war was over. She discarded the hardware and moved on.

Jenny hunted through her burrows leaving the smoking shells of drones behind her. Hunger arose between kills and waned when she killed, but it seemed to be losing its urgency. Was this because of the regular feeding? She did not know. A different kind of hunger arose after a time, but she found that feeding on the thawed out ganglions from downed drones satisfied it, and understood it had been real organic hunger and not the hunger for the kill. She deliberately did not look upon the effects of that feeding upon the human form lying within. Then came a time when she hunted through her burrows and could find no more drones. She decided then to venture to the surface and start trapping prador again, which she set about without much enthusiasm. She climbed one of the shafts leading to the surface just off the coast – choosing this location because, as far as she could assess these things, it would be the most unexpected. However, she had no doubt, that she was expected somewhere above.

Seawater filled the shaft, but that made little difference to her. When she reached the end cap, the lid, and engaged her pedipalps, to find a layer of mud above. She dug her way up through this, putting it behind her and not bothering to create a burrow. Finally oozing out in murky water she passive-scanned and was puzzled. All the indications had been, in her previous venture above, fifty kilometres further down the coast, that prador dwellings had extended into the sea. She started active scanning, carefully at first with sonar, then laser, and finally terahertz tight-beam. Nothing on the bottom for kilometres in either direction but, half a kilometre above, floated a ceiling of foamstone. Altering her buoyancy she began to float up, but suddenly the water filled with EMR and sonar detector emissions. Above she saw weapons turrets dropping through the foamstone, and cavitating beams spearing through the water towards her.

She dropped rapidly as the beams hit causing severe disruption through her body, but still she managed to get down into the mud. Since she had been detected she kept her own scanning to a maximum, and saw a long shape detach from one of the turrets and head down towards her. Fearing another neutron bomb she dug down fast to her burrow, hurling balled mud behind her, dropped inside and dragged the lid closed. Even simply dropping would not be fast enough so with a blur of limbs against the walls she also propelled herself down. A detonation above jerked her surroundings and the lid evaporated behind her. All EMR disrupted and a ceiling of fire pursued her down. She hit the bottom hard enough to make a crater, but bounced out of it and along a sagging muddy burrow. Flash-heating internal water she ejected jets of superheated steam behind and hurtled onwards, scattering decoder beads in the walls as she went. Across most of EMR she was blind. She just kept moving, hard and fast as with a rumbling all around, the fire behind her guttered and died.

The burrows had collapsed, whether from the atomic blasts or her decoders she had no idea. She slowed to a steady pace, taking the most direct route away from those blasts by memory since she still could not scan her surroundings. Slowly the EMR died and she began to inspect damage reports from within. The cavitating disruption was temporary and already fading. Fortunately the prador had not used a neutron warhead but a simple EMP and though briefly blinding its damage had been nil. The most damage she had received was from hitting the bottom of that shaft, and already her internal nanites were repairing the cracks in her composite.

She began to scan, managed to locate herself, but now wasn't sure where to go or what to do next. Then she noticed a tight terahertz beam locked on her. Informational warfare? She could sense data trying to push through, but in overview it did not seem complicated enough to be an attack, but how had something managed to do that after the recent disruption? Without opening herself to attack she inspected what she could of the thing. The bandwidth remained too low to carry effective comlife but, still, something had her located and she did not like that. She initiated chameleonware and ran, dodging through a maze of burrows, throwing out EMR ghosts of herself all around, but after an hour of this the beam remained locked on. Slowing, she decided to take a closer look at it, and allowed it access to her com-system. She identified the carrier, and the content: voice.

'Could you have been any noisier about announcing your presence down here?' the voice enquired in perfect Polity Anglic.

'Who are you?' she asked. 'What are you?'

'I'm Yellow Azimuth and I will be your guide for today, so maybe you'll get to see another one.'

'Another what?'

'Another day you moron.'

'What are you?'

'What I am is a bit pissed off right now. Reactivated, we learned. Ambush-format war drone. I thought you were supposed to be quiet and sneaky – taking down occasional prador and never revealing your presence. Twenty-six fucking war drones trashed down here is hardly what I would call quiet!'

Jenny felt oddly ashamed. 'Circumstances changed.'

'The King had this world queued up for examination and research sometime in the future since they were sure that neutron bomb did for you. But no, you had to reveal yourself on the surface and you had to be tardy with your first victim allowing it to broadcast all sorts of telemetry. Now his children are on the way down and they will not be such a walkover as the prador here or *their* drones.'

'What has happened? The King, the war?'

'First things first. I'm going to open up bandwidth a bit and send you a map – you need to get to somewhere safer.'

Jenny did not reply, but tightened down all her antiviral defences. Bandwidth opened and a map of her burrows came through. Her perception expanding with it she saw the surprisingly large extent of them. A spider icon blinked and from it a route wormed through the maze to one of the caves in which she dumped prador remains.

'Why should I trust you?' she asked.

'No particular reason at all, unless the fact that we were created by the same black AI carries some weight. Personally I would see that as a reason for greater distrust. I'll level with you: I don't want to tell you about me in case you get captured. I'm also disinclined to put myself anywhere near you just yet because I know you're fucking dangerous.'

Even though it wasn't a satisfactory answer, Jenny still found herself travelling the route mapped out.

Yellow Azimuth continued, 'And in the end, what choices do you have and what do you want to do? The lock on your programming is gone now and I'm betting the inclination to kill is fading. What's your future Jenny Trapdoor?'

'I need to know things,' she said leadenly. 'You were created by Penny Royal?'

'Indeed, and like many, and like you, my consciousness became my own once again when that AI started seeking out redemption and found apotheosis.'

'Apotheosis?'

'Keep moving, and faster than you're going now – those upper burrows are not going to be safe for much longer.'

Jenny came to a decision and accelerated. Perhaps she had been so long without talking to someone she had become naïve and easily fooled, but she felt trust in this strange 'Yellow Azimuth'.

'That's right,' said Yellow. 'Now I need to find out some things about you before we proceed and I do put myself at risk. I suggest exchanges of data. I want to see readouts from your diagnostics. I want to know what you are . . . now.'

Her trust waned a little, but she said, 'Then you start. Tell me about the war.'

'The war has been over for two centuries. The previous king of the prador was usurped and the new king forged a truce with the Polity. Now, tell me, did Penny Royal scatter pieces of itself inside you and, if so, what's happened to them?'

Jenny carried on at speed through the burrow, but automatically as her mind went into shock. Two centuries? She had been out of it for that long?

'Yeah, I guess that's a fair bit to process. I'll tell you something else while you get to grips with it. The Kingdom and the Polity are separated now by a no-man's land called the Graveyard. This world is right on the edge on the Kingdom side. Up above now they're thoroughly aware of your presence and if you go up you'll get the same reception as previously. They weren't trying to kill you – they know how difficult that would be – just driving you back down and keeping you contained until the King's children come, then –'

'Here,' Jenny interrupted, throwing a diagnostic assessment of those crystals inside her, along with her own observation of the colour change.

Yellow fell silent, but for a worryingly short time considering the amount of information she had sent. 'That's good. Nothing nasty left behind it seems. You can never be sure with Penny Royal – some of the transformed were hardly nice and hardly deserving of their portion of the redemption. Are you prepared to risk giving me a link to your diagnostics? You can limit it as much as you like.'

Jenny hesitated, but found that her doubts, her caution, her paranoia had ceased to matter. She had her life down here: going up to hunt and kill, forever in the dark – the endless repetition – but things had changed. She opened a link, and didn't bother limiting it, just as she arrived at the cave Yellow had indicated on the map. As she entered lights came on – blisters on the walls flashing on like halogen lamps. She slowed as she entered, scanning all around. Beyond the lights she could see very little untoward or different from the last time she had been in here, *two centuries ago*, but for the incrustations on the prador armour and the walls. She settled down, feeling Yellow probing back along the link and beginning to methodically to examine her systems.

'Redemption and apotheosis, you said,' she spoke to cold still air. 'What does that mean?'

'Oh, I think you know Penny Royal was fractured, mad and bad. But it grew and grew and healed those breaks. Nobody is completely sure what its aims were. It corrected many of the atrocities it had made and through various actions saved millions of lives in recompense. It then dropped itself into a black hole and went beyond time. I can feed over detail if you like?'

'Why not?' Jenny shrugged and then, on a whim because now there were lights in here, contracted her senses to the conventionally human to look around.

The tight-beam widened and began to feed her the story. Yes, Penny Royal had corrected many things, but in a way that seemed just as insane as usual – though like a god at play. She saw how it shifted the war factory Room 101 through space, converting it into a machine to take it into a black hole. She also saw how Penny Royal had been speaking from that black hole even before these actions – the indication that it had gone outside of time. The story steadily unfolded threads of meaning and further implications and they all fascinated her. Penny Royal had become something numinous and, perhaps, had always been so. The colour and detail of it expanded, fantastic, incredible, almost too painfully bright for her cave dwelling existence. It also partially swamped her perception of the diagnostic link expanding too and, too late, she moved to block it. The informational warfare hit her hard and she collapsed, folded up, just as she had when Penny Royal shut her down that time. And now, with human vision, she saw that a large patch of incrustation on the ceiling was bright yellow, as it detached like a sheet and fell upon her.

Her first was a first-child. She had opened a small system of burrows up from an underground cave, placed a sensory manifold above imbedded in the rock of a mountain slope, and kept watch. Frustratingly the prador, in the base on the shore, tended to travel through the air about their business. The only time they actually came down to the surface of this part of the continent was to hunt large four-legged arthropods. These creatures resembled bulldogs but weighed in at a couple of tons and sported wide funnel-like lamprey mouths and hooked claws on their feet. First children did this alone while second-children usually went in hunting groups of three. They did this without wearing armour and without weapons. It seemed some kind of trial, or test – as if they needed to reacquaint occasionally with their own natural weapons. In a way she understood it. She vaguely recalled s news story about a human general called Maccanan – nicknamed 'Throwback' because of his training methods. He had his recruits shut down their enhancements for training. Better soldiers were the result. Something like that, perhaps – or just some local phenomenon.

Out of old Earth traditions and memories she settled on that of the sacrificial goat. A quick ionic stun blast easily brought down one of the arthropods. Wanting no indication of a trap she could not use a rope to tie it in place. With her powerful, full EMR senses and ramped up mind, she examined the creature, and settled on an implanted device that delivered a shock every time it strayed too far from the mouth of her burrow. Weak signalling between her and that device should not be detected, especially since the hunters did not wear their armour with all its enhancements.

She waited, for days and days and then weeks, her hunger increasing and gnawing at her until it became painful. Then the first-child came. She detected it primarily through the sensory manifold, skimming over the mountains in its suit. It circled overhead, seeing the big arthropod – Jenny had taken care to select one of the larger ones. After a short time the first-child landed a couple of kilometres away, but still within range of the manifold. There it raised the top half of its armour on chromed rods and hinged it over. Air blasts and plungers lifted the creature up out of its suit and it nimbly hurled itself to one side to land on soft soil. Seeing it through the manifold like this, brought lubricating fluids drooling from her fangs. Of course, Penny Royal had ensured salivation.

  The first-child stalked close, pausing on a nearby ridge to observe the arthropod. It then worked its way down the slope attempting to conceal itself by moving quickly from one patch of thick coiled tubular leaves to another. It was almost comedic that something so large was trying to stay hidden and, the arthropods being apex predators they tended never to run away but towards. Jenny felt no amusement – her hunger had grown too intense. As the prador approached, the arthropod, having received another shock at the boundary Jenny had set, returned and even walked back over the lid of her burrow. She found herself having to fight instinct not to flip the lid back and grab the thing. The prador eased out from behind another clump of those coiled leaves, then leapt out into the open with its claws raised high and open, and charged. The arthropod turned, confused by the shocks it received and, rather than charging to meet the prador as usual for its kind, it emitted a plaintive whistling and gurgling. The prador slowed, hesitated, and Jenny cursed it. But in the end it too was a predator and, though it sensed something strange here, it stalked forward.

  Far enough. . .

  Jenny flipped up the lid and came fast out of her burrow. She knocked the arthropod aside and grabbed the prador, but with hooked feet skittering on its carapace, lost her grip. Thankfully, rather than retreat, the prador attacked her, closing claws on her legs. She dragged it back with her towards the burrow. Unable to snip through her legs it released one claw and went for her eyes. She ducked that instinctively, even though it had little chance of harming her. The claw still hit, but skittered off adamantine materials. The prador must have realised it was up against something very dangerous, so released its other claw and tried to retreat. Jenny wanted it in her burrow, but her need to feed overwhelmed that.

She leapt and came down on the thing, grabbing again. A claw came up under her head, fending her off, but she increased the pressure, driving it down, and got her fangs to carapace, chain diamond rims screaming. The fangs went into carapace easily, spattering saliva soaked dust all around, and with a final crack she punched inside the thing. The prador shrieked and bubbled, mandibles clashing. It struggled and thrashed in exquisite agony as she injected digestive juices. She held it, scanning deep as its struggles continued, seeing all the soft internal components of this living creature dissolving. Her first sip of the juices flowed into her like cold water after days trekking across a desert, like a hit of heroin to an addict, like a gulp of whisky to an alcoholic. The ecstasy of it had her shivering and jerking, and it just seemed to grow as she tilted and shifted, hoovering up more, sucking down chunks of half-dissolved organ too, and as the prador's struggles died.

Finally, the prador sucked dry, she pulled out her fangs and let it collapse loose-limbed to the ground. Now she felt more thoroughly organic as if that component of her, now being fed, had asserted dominance within her. She settled back, still quivering, just as the arthropod slammed into her side. Almost without thinking she pushed it away, but simultaneously initiated a punch laser in her foot. The arthropod collapsed with fire licking out of carapace joints, then a steady growing cloud of black smoke began to rise from it. Jenny just stared at it, revelling in pleasure, but as that began to fade her intellect began to reassert. She needed to clear up.

Quickly now, Jenny dragged the prador over to her burrow and dropped it down inside. After a moment's thought she did the same with the arthropod. Stupid to have killed her lure like that but, then, she felt this method of trapping prador was far too slow. Now, having experienced feeding, she did not want to wait so long to do so again. Next she went fast up the slope, over the ridge and to the prador's armour, grabbed that and dragged it to her burrow too. During the return journey she thought about vengeance, about this payback for Gogh, for the destruction of her ship and all the people aboard, and for what had happened to her, but it just seemed a rote almost mathematical accounting. Feeding held much more importance. Closing the lid behind her and heading down, she dragged the remains to that underground cave. And then, she paused, as a weird feeling rippled out from deep inside her and it felt . . . almost human.

Jenny turned her attention inward trying to trace the source of that feeling. It did not emanate from her extended processing, or her internal sensors and spider nervous system so, with a degree of distaste she focused on her human remains. Something had changed. First she noticed the feed from her altered human digestive system fat with nutrients heading back to replenish the semi-organics of her spinnerets, and the same fattening in her web as that inner body distributed other semi-organics throughout, like to the organ in which she created her digestive juices. Was this topping up of resources the source of the sensation? No, it came from her remains. She studied them closely and now saw the change. A gel had filled up the spaces in the body mould, and through that she could blood-fed strips of muscle had appeared on her printed ribcage. She abruptly retreated from that because, somehow, it seemed obscene. Everything about her, of course, had been made by that insane AI, and it seemed she had discovered another insanity – a fraction of the nutrients she ate being used to regrow her human body, forever trapped inside. She shivered, trying to dismiss questions about why and further ones about where this might lead, and turned her attention outwards again.

She examined and deactivated the systems in the prador armour and, even while dealing with that felt her hunger starting to nag again – those nutrient stores needed to be filled. She tried to extract more juice from inside the armour and managed a sip or two, tried feeding on the arthropod but then spewed out what she took just a moment later in disgust. She needed to get proactive now. She needed to extend her network, install more sensory manifolds, and work out how best to grab more prador, more quickly.

She needed to feed. She kept that thought firmly at the forefront of her mind, and found it easier now to suppress those earlier questions.

The paralysis faded and, internally she could see and feel silvery nanoscopic threads detaching from the packed technology and organics of her, out to the yellow sheet that had closed over her as tightly as prador armour. She began to be able to move. Everything that she was started to come back online as the sheet slid off her, along the floor like a shifting wash of yellow paint, then up one wall where it spread out like a 2D representation of a neuron.

'Well Penny Royal certainly did a number on you,' said Yellow Azimuth. 'But in one sense you're lucky – it seems one of the good fragments of Penny Royal's mind had its input into your construction.'

'Good fragments?' she managed.

'I cannot quite plumb your perception of that AI so I'll explain.' The sheet rippled slightly, a tight spiral of wrinkles appearing that Jenny felt sure must be a grimace. 'Penny Royal was a fractured AI with personality fragments constantly seeking dominance overall. Even when it was working on something the influence of various fragments waxed and waned. It seemed that nasty fragments turned you into a voracious predator on prador, while nice ones managed to insert the possibility of a way out for you.'

'You make no sense. I am what I am.'

'And what you are,' said Yellow, 'is so disgusted and even horrified by your human remains that you blocked them out of your mind, though I concede that the nasty parts of Penny Royal probably influenced that. It strikes me as likely they could not do anything about the physical changes to the spider system, so twisted your mind to reject them instead.'

'You still make no sense,' said Jenny, feeling panic rising inside her.

'Don't you wonder why the quadruple amputee you were was installed in a mould of a complete human? Perhaps you should take a look, since you haven't done so in a long time.'

Panic turned to anger, and she wanted to strip Yellow from the wall and burn it down to nothing. But pushing up from under that, out of her distributed computing, arose hard logical analysis. Yellow was correct. She tried to turn her attention inward again to inspect those remains, but ended up fighting herself. She glimpsed something bloody, ropes of muscle and bare white tendon, and abruptly retreated. The panic began to wane, the anger too. She would look again sometime – when she felt ready – and, with amused self-deprecation acknowledge that she herself was Penny Royal in microcosm with parts of her mind at war with each other.

'And you,' she said, escaping uncomfortable self-examination both physical and mental. 'Penny Royal made you, too, so what the hell are you?'

Yellow Azimuth shifted and speared out two extensions around the wall. 'Is it not obvious? I am paint.'

'What?'

'As an artist I was particularly noted for my specially designed vacuum nanopaints and the use of yellow in my paintings. One of my most famous creations was of an alien sunrise given my particular twist.'

'I don't understand.'

'I was a Golem android and took my art as far as I could go it that form – travelling the Polity and trying different techniques, different lifestyles in my quest to create superior art. Penny Royal shattered my crystal into nanoscopic shreds and distributed me through my paint. I could create art, like this. . .'

Yellow shifted and began to form a pattern of yellows turning like a kaleidoscope image and taking on three-dimensional depth. Jenny could feel herself falling into something wonderful and weird and began walking towards it. Then as it shredded and faded she felt a surge of nostalgia for a lost beauty she could never describe. But as she came out of this she sensed holes in Yellow's story – an edited down version for her consumption.

'But of course, as had always been the way with Penny Royal, the cost exceeded the gain. I could create but even in reflection or in recorded image I could never see my own creations. I went insane for the best part of a century and, when I started trying to form myself around people to try and see through their eyes what I was, and left them stripped of their own skin and screaming, ECS managed to capture me and confine me in a flask in one of their vaults.'

'And why are you not there now?'

'Redemption.'

'A word you seem fond of.'

'Twenty years ago one of the fragments of black crystal within me, for I had them just the same as you, grew and extended into a spine, penetrating the flask. I escaped and found that I could now see myself, though my sanity and much of my mind was gone. The spine shattered and reintegrated. Over ensuing years I could feel Penny Royal making corrections and now I am redeemed. I cannot remember my name or much of my life, so I have taken the name of that last sunrise: Yellow Azimuth.'

'But surely you can find out who you were?' Jenny's tone was flat, devoid of any hint that she had detected lies.

'I can, and perhaps one day I will, but in doing so I must venture into Polity AI networks and that is something I have no inclination for yet.'

Another lie. . .

'There is danger there then, for you and I?'

'Oh yes. Penny Royal righted some wrongs. But the Polity AIs recognise it as something appallingly powerful and dangerous, and they will never let any of its creations go unexamined to the nth degree.'

'So what now?

'Is there anything further you need to know?'

'Just the exigencies of now – these King's children. . .'

'Are now down on the surface of the world. Would you like to see them?'

'You have a network up there . . . I lost mine.'

'The sensory manifolds you deployed, and were about to deploy again I see since you have some inside you, had a limited life.'

'Let me see.'

The link came through from Yellow and she opened it. In her mind a network expanded much like her own and in a flash she noted the location of viewpoints from all her burrow exits. She shuffled through these eagerly, building up a picture of the planet above, and then that extending out to viewpoints in orbit. The two continents were like two commas turned against each other, but one of them much smaller. Ocean between them was clear of anything, but chains of islands spread out from them matching the curves of their coasts like echoes. Amalgamating views and extrapolations she saw the large prador towns extended along the coasts, but now many sections of the oceanic component of them floated on the surface rather than lay along the bottom as before.

'The ocean sections are easily raised or lowered,' Yellow informed her, and now she could feel its presence as she had once felt Penny Royal, but it did not seem dangerous or beyond her comprehension. 'They keep them on the bottom when volcanic activity here generates tsunamis and raise them at other times. This time they raised them because of you, while in the shore sections they abandoned the lower living quarters and in the upper had armed prador and drones with seismic detectors.'

'An excessive response?' Jenny suggested.

'Not really, after you wiped out all those drones.'

'You used the past tense.'

'The King told them to return to life as normal and merely drive you back down if you appear. They were instructed not to use any of the neutron warheads they were lining up. He doesn't want them to hunt or kill you and, to be frank, does not care how many prador you kill here.'

'Why?'

'For the same reason the Polity AIs want you: because you're dangerous and he wants to capture and study you.'

Jenny grunted an acknowledgement of that.

Now she noticed that between the shore towns massive breakwaters extended out to capture mud flats swarming with creatures like giant mud skippers. Upon seeing these she took a view out over the ocean and there saw chequerboard patterns of fish farms and did not need to look too closely to know the pens would be full of reaverfish. So that was what had happened here.

When she first came to this world it sat on the edge of the prador kingdom and, now with this 'Graveyard' borderland still did. Then the world had obviously only recently been occupied, with little sign of a long-established prador population, but it later acquired large war camps and weapons facilities, it being one stepping stone, one supply line to the war with the Polity. Now she saw that the world seemed devoid of weapons installations and the big factories in the middle of the smaller continent, where they had not fallen into dilapidation, seemed to have been converted into stockyards for beasts resembling six-legged cattle.

'I would have expected more of a military presence this close to this Graveyard?' she queried.

'They have this,' Yellow replied, running a feed to her that took her out across the reaches of vacuum to a space station resembling an iron Brazil nut, but bristling with weapons and perhaps twenty kilometres long. 'The border on both sides of the Graveyard is scattered with forts like this. Also, lessons of war have taught both sides that planet-based military installations are too vulnerable. The big stuff stays out in space. Like these. . .'

Back to the planet now and she saw numerous weaponised satellites and space stations around it. There were ships too: three recognisable prador dreadnoughts of the style she had seen before, so probably ancient and dated, and five polished looking things like extended teardrops each a few miles long, their metal golden.

'Those?'

'Reavers,' Yellow explained. 'What the King's children arrived in. In fact you can see more of those children heading down to the planet now.'

Jenny focused in to see shuttles descending, but also around them numerous armoured prador descending on grav. Though a familiar sight from the past she discerned something different. They all seemed to be the size of first-children, but with sleeker and highly-coloured armour covered in patterns and unusual designs.

'I didn't know the prador had artists too,' she commented.

'They didn't until the end of the war and the rise of the new king and his children.'

'No, I mean I didn't think them even capable of art.'

'They weren't and many still aren't, but the King and his children are different.'

'Why?'

'You know about the human blanks,' said Yellow. It wasn't a question but a statement of fact. This confirmed for Jenny just how deeply Yellow – who was effectively an AI of the distributed swarm variety – had penetrated her previously. It probably knew much of her history, and had copied memories it could access in a moment.

'Yes. . .'

'You know something of Jay Hoop and his pirates on the planet they came from, and something of the virus occupying their bodies. But, you have been utterly incurious for a long time, and never really considered the questions that virus poses. Perhaps think about that now.'

Just beyond the south coast lay a perfect hunting ground and she had burrows scattered all the way along it. The downside of this was the instability of the seabed, what with it being a mixture of worm-eaten limestone, conglomerate and clay, and subject to frequent seismic activity. Periods of burrow repair often interrupted her hunting there, since they kept collapsing.

Prador were predators, hunters, and they frequently ventured out into the sea in search of the large fish-like creatures of this world. These resembled barracuda, but for the trilateral symmetry of their heads, which had three-jawed mouths, three eyes and three fronds to detect organics in the water. Again the prador set out after these only in their natural armour, though they did sport spear guns. Having speared a number of these creatures they towed some back to their homes but left others nearer to the coast, anchored to the bottom. This activity, related to her objectives of hunting and killing prador, also stirred her waning curiosity. It was a novel thing to feel. She opened a burrow into one of their shore bases and introduced a sensory manifold there. The fish they brought back the prador put through lengthy processing to make their flesh edible. The final dried and vacuum-sealed result went into crates heading for the space port slab. A taste of the alien to be sold to other prador? She had ascertained that they did have an exchange system running and did use money in the form of laminar diamond crystals. But she had yet to see any leisure pursuits amidst them beyond hunting – it all seemed to be about power, accruing resources and killing enemies. Perhaps they were gourmands? Thoughts along these lines caused brief discomfort to arise, as she understood herself to be little different now.

Why they left other fish anchored to the bottom remained a mystery until the first hatching. Via her manifolds she saw what she thought of as corpses steadily expanding, then one of them began thrashing as if it had come alive. On closer inspection – peering inside the creature – she saw that it was alive, and very much not liking what was happening inside it. She saw numerous hatching eggs scattered throughout its body. The things that came out were much like fish themselves, though with hooked fins to tow them through their hosts as they fed. As the host died they bored out through the skin, then these 'fry' shoaled about the corpse and dined on the remains. Jenny checked the other fish and saw that they were alive and similarly infested. She then began to check data she had yet to delete from the manifolds as being useless to her purposes. She now saw that the fish taken back for processing had been dead, while these ones had been hit with tail shots that did not kill them. It seemed evident the prador had used a paralytic. She then saw, when the prador were anchoring them, that they had injected these eggs. She ventured out of her burrow for the unusual activity of satisfying curiosity and snared some of the fry. Close examination revealed them to be the juvenile version of the prador reaverfish – one of their food animals. She wondered briefly how they had been modified to this alien environment, but by then her hunger was growing again and consequently the brief spurt of curiosity dying.

Along the coast she grabbed prador at a rate of one every few weeks at far separate locations. This seemed maintainable since the father-captains had very little regard for their children and certainly some were injured or killed by the trihead fishes. But after ten weeks the prador started to head out in tight, almost military-formation hunting parties, and began wearing their armour. She pulled back inland and began taking them in a series of areas where they hunted the arthropods. Her kills were sparse there and, after a time, the hunters started donning armour. She still took them – the armour being no real barrier to her – but later on the hunting just stopped. She returned to her burrows along the coast, finding recent earthquakes had collapsed most of them. She opened some out, but found the hunting here had died out too. In desperation she opened more burrows in and around the coastal bases – taking some that ventured outside on foot, and even taking some in their own dwellings. By now, out of fear generated by dying opportunities to hunt, she was using her manifolds to monitor prador communications. They knew something was wrong – that something was killing them down here. She heard speculation about an as yet unidentified life form. To prevent discovery she started making burrows out to the occupied islands and tried to limit her predation. But then, in just one night, events dispelled all her concerns.

Her manifolds first alerted her to large shuttles arriving – more than the small spaceport slab could support. It delighted her to see shuttles landing all across the continents and across the sea, and prador disembarking. Her delight rose to new heights when she saw the swarms of them descending on the grav in their armour from huge ships that had appeared in orbit. She watched them constructing bases and weapons installations but, feeding regularly on this new crop, it never even occurred to her to wonder about the reason for all this, until a projectile hit one of the dreadnoughts with force enough to spread it as fiery twisted metal in a comet-like line across the night sky. Since she had no manifolds out in space she could only see events up there from the surface. However, combining all of them gave her telescopic resolution. She saw an approaching war runcible annihilated by prador dreadnoughts, and she saw the Polity fleet engaging. Did this mean the Polity were winning, having now penetrated into the Kingdom? She thought not. The Polity ships seemed more rugged now and had weapons that could damage prador ships, but the prador still had the advantage and were taking an appalling toll on this attacking fleet.

Night became day as this warfare spread across the sky. During the day the sky swarmed with activity in silhouette. Jenny joyfully grabbed prador that wandered close to her burrow caps on the surface, and never grew hungry day after day for weeks. The warfare up there then moved in closer to the world. Debris fell through atmosphere – some huge chunks opening craters that shook the ground, or creating tsunamis equal to those this world created naturally. Next came the orbital strikes. She saw new ground installations ejecting hardfield generators in molten explosions across the surface. She saw the seas along the coasts boiling from heat sinks recently anchored to the bottom. When one of the bases failed under this assault and disappeared in a sun bright explosion, she looked to the skies resentfully, because the Polity was killing her prey. This resentment increased when more accurate strikes began to take out armoured prador in the sky and, up there, she saw drones, nominally of her own kind, at war.

These, along with human troops in atmosphere entry shells, began to arrive on the surface. Jenny, busily repairing her burrow system because the orbital railgun strikes penetrated deep, watched them through her manifolds when interference wasn't too severe. She soon surmised that they were aiming to bring down the base defences so they could be destroyed from orbit. During the battles that ensued she grabbed more prey, and more still. Next, as the vacuum warfare began dying and along with it the massive EMR interference, she probed the spectrum searching for information, though mostly on where she could next grab prey. As she did this she found the Polity data sphere around the world but, unfortunately, its defensive datavores and hounds began hunting her. Later she penetrated with more caution, but still only to locate prey. It never occurred to her to question all this activity until Polity forces actually invaded her territory.

Jenny did not need sensory manifolds down in her burrows. The map of them was etched in her mind and, through the nano-silk she sensed them almost as part of her, and in detail. She had become aware of the interlopers but, having recently fed and feeling somnolent, had not responded. Some hours passed until someone lifted one her of burrow caps and its sensors automatically activated, also linking into the nano-silk web. Now, rising again to the state of readiness to kill, she felt affronted. She headed tentatively towards that location, then faster and faster, with her senses going to full alert and data input from the nano-silk rising.

'Something is coming,' said a voice.

She halted and listened intently.

'Has to be one of you – you saw that back there.'

Now thoroughly alert and tuned in through the nano-silk and through the burrow cap sensors, she observed the invaders. Four appeared to be human, though readings from two indicated they might not be – quite likely they were Golem. One of the humans was closing the end cap, obviously having taken a look above. They were heavily armed and armoured and had been towing a large mine on a sled. Two mosquito autoguns accompanied them, but also a drone in the form of a giant chromed lobster near to Jenny's size. What she could scan of the thing showed it to be similarly equipped to her. It even seemed to have volumes of dense tech within, almost as integrated as hers. She also noted an absence. This creature had no space within it occupied by bloody irrelevant organics, but a mind of crystal, like Penny Royal.

Only retrospectively, as she continued to tune nano-silk and glean data, did she trace the invasion. They had entered one of her burrows through the wall of a newly-formed debris crater. They had followed her burrows heading nominally towards the prador base lying just a few kilometres away from their present location. Along their route had been one of her mortuary caves, so they had seen the prador remains there.

'Not necessarily,' replied the drone flatly. 'We have no data on any drones penetrating the Kingdom or being sent to this world. It could be some life form we haven't seen before.'

'Yeah, but the armour...'

'Anything we can do, life can do,' the drone mused.

'You're shitting me. Draphen here analysed that stuff. The holes were made with chain diamond cutters, two we saw were killed with a high intensity laser, one with a railgun strike to its rear end and some of the other damage looked like hardfield shear.'

'Yeah, you got me.'

'So what the fuck is it?'

'Something above your pay grade. Take the mine and place it, then get out of this burrow system just as fast as you can. I'll put myself between you and it.'

'Rogue?' asked the man.

'Something like that.'

'So dangerous?' the man insisted.

'You saw the prador,' the drone pointed out.

The man grunted annoyance, obviously aware he would get no further.

Rare curiosity arose again and Jenny stalked closer. She also stalked closer in the informational realm – probing, searching and snatching data from under the noses of the vores and hounds. This time it seemed surprisingly easy to gain access, and only later did she understand why. As the data began to build in her mind, and integrated with stuff she had taken on other occasions, she understood some things. The four were a Sparkind unit consisting of two humans and two Golem – a standard for Polity Special Forces now. Probing identities she hit a mother-lode of information on the drone: its war record. It was out of Room 101 and like many drones from that War Factory had been non-standard from the start and had swiftly, during ensuing conflicts, diverged along its own developmental path. She had no doubt it had been made with technology gifted to the War Factory AI by Penny Royal. Simple mission parameters she found linked: a directed contra-terrene explosion under the base to destroy it. And now she did wonder about the objectives here. Yes, they were damaging the prador but it seemed at huge cost, for there seemed nothing to be gained other than smashing Polity forces to pieces against adamantine prador defences.

'I know you can hear me,' said the drone.

'And you can hear me?' Jenny asked.

'I hear you.' The drone swivelled to face up the burrow along which Jenny approached. Its body clicked and hissed and things whined up to power – all with the feel of breach blocks clicking home.

'Why are you here?' Jenny asked.

'You have seen: Just to take out the base the guys are now heading for. Once they're done we'll get out of your burrows and no one will be coming down here again. No need to get . . . tetchy.'

Jenny now understood that the drone had allowed her penetration of the data sphere. 'No. Why is the Polity here, expending so many ships and troops against this world? It is . . . wasteful.'

The drone seemed to settle a bit, but she was thoroughly aware that its weapons remained active. 'Strategy. An attack here draws off prador troops and ships from other locations. One of those locations, now sufficiently weakened, is about to get splashed.'

'I see.'

'Do you indeed. I'm surprised you care.'

'What do you mean?'

'We know what you are and who made you. . .'

'I have been given the power to exact revenge. I have my reasons for killing prador.'

'Yeah, sure you do.'

The drone's attitude annoyed her, but what annoyed her further was the breach of a promise it had made. She advanced along the burrow, finally bringing the drone into line of sight. The predator, arising in her with sickening intensity, had her wanting to attack, but part of her that always remained separate, questioned that and she just froze, railgun ready, all weapons ready.

'You promised,' she said.

'I see what you see,' said the drone. 'They are not ours.'

'They are human. . .' Through the nano-silk she could see twenty of them had come in where this drone and the other four had entered. She studied them closely. They wore weapons harnesses over ragged ill-maintained clothing. She noted a bluish tinge to their skin and numerous keratinous scars over their bodies.

'They are blanks,' said the drone.

'I don't understand.'

'I imagine your sensory capabilities are as good as if not better than mine down here. Look inside them.'

Jenny hesitated, felt that surge again and took a few skittering paces forwards. The drone backed up a little, but protruded a square section barrel from its mouth. She forced restraint and did as the drone had suggested. Through the nano-silk she looked inside the twenty as she had looked inside the drone here. For a moment she felt as if her probe was being blocked but then realised that the human bodies, though possessing the requisite organs, were as dense and fibrous as old wood. Then she looked into their skulls. There she found no sign of the organs that should occupy them but instead metallic prador thrall technology.

'What is this?'

'Since you're looking there anyway, here it is.'

Information access further opened for her in the data sphere as the vores retreated but remained watchful. She snatched it and loaded it at once. She had seen prador putting their thrall hardware in some animals, and in some of their children. In less rugged life forms like humans it should not have been possible but, on a particularly watery world was a virus that turned humans into tough reusable food resources for the main creature that carried the virus – leeches. And humans, treacherous piratical humans, were capturing other humans, infecting them with the virus and selling them to the prador as hosts for this hardware. She felt disgusted with humanity. She felt they did not deserve to win against the prador. Only weakly, on a low level, did she have it in mind that she had once been human too. The thought then arose that she still was, at her core, but she mentally skittered away from that. She turned, processing the seized data, and suppressing a rare feeling of panic, as she mapping out a route to intercept these interlopers.

'I'll go this way,' said the drone, injecting a map into the data sphere. Timings were there too. They would intercept these 'blanks' in the mortuary chamber along their route. It didn't matter to her whether the drone would be there or not. She would kill these creatures, and then she would collapse her burrows around that crater, and allow no one down here again.

Jenny moved fast through her burrows, the intensity of her kill instinct growing. She tracked the twenty, noting that they were armed like the Polity soldiers, but not armoured. She made assessments – if they could withstand prador thrall technology then their bodies had to be very tough. Go for the technology, then. . .

Finally she came to a turning, slowed as if in preparation and then realising she needed none, surged round the corner and into the mortuary chamber. The twenty, she saw, moved in much the same way, heads turning from side to side in a rippling pattern that took in their surroundings as a whole. She saw the pause, then the heads all turning towards her. There was an operator – a prador – and an appreciable delay in their actions. They began to aim their weapons, but by that time she was amongst them. All punch lasers operating she took four of them at once, burning fist-wide holes into the backs of their skulls. The beams from laser carbines intersected on her, etching across her armour as she sent another two tumbling. Another beam lanced in – deep blue particle beam with an odd violet tint – punching through the same targets she had aimed for, and bringing another four down in quick succession. She found her movements impeded as some of the blanks hung onto her with enormous strength. Even though these weren't her usual prey she hit three of them with her fangs, injecting digestive enzymes and retracting. A moment later the drone was in amongst it too, snipping with its claws and lashing out with that particle beam.

She fired her railgun, recoil sending her skidding back, the projectile exploding through two blanks. Bouncing off the wall she hurtled back, bit and lashed out, turned thrall tech to smoking molten metal with her punch lasers.

The drone retreated, dragging one of the blanks with it, just as she sensed a distant blast. She ignored it and continued her killing spree. Those whose thrall hardware she destroyed she saw still moving. But now they weren't fighting with any coordination, just thrashing at her and seeming to have lost the ability to wield their weapons.

'Operator in the base,' said the drone, returning and dumping the blank it had taken, now headless, down with the rest. Jenny turned slowly. No more of them were standing. Those she had bitten were thrashing and crawling with their bodies coming apart.

'These need to be disposed of,' said the drone.

It fired up its particle cannon again, wide beam, and began burning the blanks. Jenny hesitated for a second, then fired up her lasers, burning the still moving dead people too, Soon the mortuary chamber filled with fire, smoke and blackening human remains. She faced the drone in an inferno that touched neither of them.

'Leave,' she said.

The drone tilted its head, turned away.

'I hope, one day, you escape this Hell,' it said. 'In seems the option is inside you.'

The comments seemed apposite – her standing amidst the flames – but she had no idea what they meant. Anyway, though she had enjoyed the kills here, they had been not been satisfying. It was time to collapse those burrows exposed by the crater, and then go up to grab more prador from the surface.

The memory had risen unbidden and in exquisite detail. She felt her anger at the humans who had captured other humans and sold them to the prador and still retained all the data she had grabbed so long ago from the Polity data sphere. Before, she had just scanned across it, but now she looked into it more deeply and questions truly did begin to occur. Alien bugs could infect humans with results that were either indifferent or disastrous. Either the human body killed them or they fed on it voraciously, finally killing it. But it was all about feeding and nothing about supplanting human cellular machinery or doing any of the things viruses and bacteria did on Earth, because the alien bugs had not evolved alongside the humans. That an alien virus could occupy a human, turn it into a reusable food resource and so thoroughly alter physiognomy was, well, highly unlikely.

'Yes, I have questions,' she said, but needed to say no more than that because it seemed Yellow was still as much in her mind as she was.

'The virus is an eclectic collector of genomes but, up until about five million years ago, only of the genomes of the creatures on Spatterjay.'

That was all the paintshop AI said – it just waited for her to work some things out. Five million years ago usually meant only one thing.

'Jain technology,' she said.

'In a word: yes. Five million years ago, for reasons that simply cannot be elucidated, a squad of Jain biomechs transcribed themselves into the genome of the Spatterjay virus. Maybe it was to be turned into a weapon. Maybe it was so they could hide and come back, reborn from the virus at a later time. But things got highly disrupted and it is difficult for that Jain genome to express. However, it has resulted in the virus being able to adapt to alien life forms – all alien life forms.'

Jenny got it at once as she gazed upon the descending prador. 'What did it do to them?'

'Physically they have changed in many ways and are as difficult to kill as those human blanks you and that drone burned up down here. Mentally it has boosted their intelligence. We can attribute the end of the war directly to the virus. A father-captain was infected and became smart enough to realise that the prador war effort was doomed against AI production . . . doomed against the productive might of places like war factory Room 101. Also infecting his children he went back to the Kingdom, usurped the then king and immediately negotiated a truce with the Polity. In essence he saved the prador kingdom. If the war had continued the Polity would have broken it and thereafter confined surviving prador to the surfaces of their worlds.'

'So these children of the new king are dangerous,' said Jenny.

'Damned right.'

'So how do we get out of here?'

The words had risen out of her quite naturally and, retrospectively, she realised she had changed immensely. She had not felt angered by the invasiveness of Yellow. Her hunger, in reality, had been steadily waning since she exited that water cavern. And now a universe of the possible lay open to her. Hunting and killing prador no longer had to be her main purpose, her main aim, though she had yet to divine what that might be, or could be.

'Well,' said Yellow. 'When you're a mass of nanomachines concealment is easy. For example, did you not wonder how I so easily kept track of you?'

Jenny rapidly began inspecting herself, but before finding anything, Yellow said, 'Rear left quarter of your abdomen – about a centimetre across.'

Having three-sixty degree vision it was easy for Jenny to focus there. The tracker Yellow had put on her just looked like a spot of paint, which it of course was, in a sense, basically.

'When did you put that there?' she asked.

'I have those spotted all over this world and up in orbit,' said Yellow. 'They act for me like your sensory manifolds. Knowing about you I quickly found all your burrow caps and put one on each. They are as mobile as me of course. They are me. I stuck myself on you as you left that undersea burrow.' Yellow paused contemplatively then added, 'I must take in some more mass because I won't be collecting them up when we leave here. But later, much later.'

'I think you've strayed from the point,' said Jenny dryly.

'Oh yeah. Well, concealment is easy for me – I don't have to be yellow you know.' With that the paint AI changed colour and just disappeared from sight for a moment, before returning seemingly brighter than before. 'However, concealment is not so easy when you're and eight ton mechanical spider.'

'And by and by you will get to the point. . .'

'Well, the way to escape from here is to give yourself up.'

After wreaking destruction at the cost of an appalling amount of ships and fighters, the Polity fleet retreated. It wasn't an ordered retreat but a messy one. From her burrows, through her array of manifolds, she watched the fleet trying to hold a line to allow slower and more damaged ships to get away, and then finally, in one of those AI cold calculations, having to abandon their fellows.

The same occurred down on the planet. She watched troops trying to escape in shuttles and singularly with grav harnesses. The drones tried to keep the prador back but were too few to be completely effective. And anyway, when many of those escaping the surface reached orbit, ships were not available to take them aboard. She then watched humans, Golem and drones flinging themselves out into vacuum while the prador hunted. Through the collapsing data sphere she discovered the strategy of these survivors: all were shutting themselves down as they sped away from the planet. The Golem and drones were dropping themselves to minimal power usage while the humans were using hibernation tech in their suits. All were hoping to one day be dredged up out of interstellar space. Few of them made it as the prador hunted them down.

Some remained on the surface and simply fought on until the prador slaughtered them – usually running in heavy war machines on caterpillar treads then themselves hitting the survivors. None of the Polity forces, she noticed, allowed capture. The humans, when faced with that, blew all their munitions at once, usually as close as possible to the nearest prador. She surmised that beyond the fact that prador had signed no conventions on the treatment of prisoners, and generally enjoyed eating them alive, there was the likelihood of them being turned into creatures like those she and the drone had burned up in her burrows. Golem and drones fought until utterly immobilised, then blew power supplies. She felt some sense of the tragedy of it all penetrate her and, unusually, found herself planning kills that assisted those remaining troops. But in the end they all died, every last one of them.

A prador clean-up operation ensued. Out in vacuum she saw prador returning with suited humans they had snared up. Through prador communications, now the Polity data sphere was gone, she learned of their failure to take these humans as prisoners. The moment they tried to open those space suits, explosives detonated. She watched the prador then expelling the would-be captives from their ships towards the planet, to burn up on re-entry. Other space debris, after some attempts at salvage, they treated similarly. It seemed the Polity did not want the prador to learn anything from the wrecked technology and had filled it with booby traps.

On the surface the prador then dozered wreckage into craters and buried it. They built new bases, while armaments factories began to spring up. It seemed that in the logistics and strategy of the war this world had become more important and a larger prador military presence being established. As last traces of the conflict disappeared, so too did Jenny's thoughts on it. Her focus closed down to the fact that there were a lot more prador here now – a lot more prey. Solstan years passed with the busyness of war supply occupying large areas of the surface above. They were bountiful years for Jenny as she filled her underground caverns with prador remains. However, somewhere in the accounting, in the logistics, the steady loss of prador first- and second-children was noted. The prador became constantly vigilant – searching the oceans and the land surface – but yet to probe below that surface. As from the beginning the nano-silk defeated most conventional scanning. Perhaps it was their constant inability to find her, or perhaps it was simply how many she had killed and how easily, but an arrogance arose. Or perhaps it was that her usual prey did not satisfy as much as they once did. Or complacency – even that.

Jenny penetrated one of their shore bases, weaving her burrows between prador burrows, mapping it all out. She found a steady increase in defences towards the core of the base and, unusually, brought more of her Penny Royal gifted facilities online and steadily worked her way through them. As expected, she found an inner sanctum, and running nano-silk through foamstone and between laminated slabs of armour and detectors, she peered inside.

The father-captain was much like many she had seen on the surface or up in space, though, always they had been surrounded by many of their children, all heavily armed. He had lost his legs, claws and mandibles and replaced them with prosthetics. The claws and mandibles were working copies rendered in a hard golden metal. Unusually, however, he had not given himself mobility with grav engines, but a series of telescopic protrusions from the leg sockets ending in caterpillar treads and wheels. From this she assumed him to be very old, and had lost his limbs before grav engines became the standard replacement. Salivating, Jenny steadily burrowed her way through the defences, decohered armour, turned foamstone to dust, usurped sensors. This work was even slower and more methodical than usual for her. Many times she retreated from it to grab prador children elsewhere to quell her hunger, though that did not seem as good as the promise that lay ahead.

Finally reaching the inner layer around the sanctum she retreated and made other preparation. She did not want to leave such a prize behind, so she expanded one burrow way down to a mortuary cavern. Then she was ready.

Jenny cut round, making a hatch and binding it in place in two sections with nano-silk. As she did this she felt a growing background of puzzlement to her main thinking. Certainly, she felt that feeding on a father-captain would be different and more satisfying but she was taking such huge risks here. What else did she hope to gain? Finally, she cut the silk on one side to drop the hatch, and now nothing lay between her and her prey.

'I have come for you,' she said, in perfect prador clatter-speech. Again that puzzlement, since she had never talked to any of her victims before.

'What are you?' he asked, though the speech had its elements of expletives, surprise and fear.

'Your death,' she replied.

He spun round on his treads, wheels scarring across the walls and tilted back to see her properly. At once Gatling cannons on his back opened fire, and then antipersonnel lasers. She dropped through the storm, railgun firing once, its recoil diverting her course and its shot shearing through two telescopic limbs. Damage reports arose for her inspection – the lasers had a softening effect and the Gatling slugs were armour-piercers railed out with incredible force. Bouncing off a wall she extruded more of her own weapons, targeting all his prosthetics and weapons. Another railgun shot took off one claw and the father-captain emitted a bubbling scream. Her own slug throwers smashed the lasers as a third railgun shot took out one of the cannons. Then she was down on him with punch lasers, lashing out and destroying weapons all around her. The father-captain accelerated and smashed into a wall. He got a claw up to one of her back legs and shear fields initiated along its inner faces, cutting in. Jenny tried to get her fangs in, but his carapace was thick and laminated through with armour, and such his frenzy he kept jouncing her out of place.

Meanwhile she was scanning through manifolds she had planted in the base, and now saw his children on the move – heading fast towards the sanctum. Huge heavy doors began to open on one side. She threw herself clear of him and, already having scanned and assessed everything here, fired a single railgun shot into the wall, smashing the door mechanism and freezing them in place open just a metre wide. A moment later he rammed into her with the edge of his carapace, smashing her into a wall. Damage reports began to red-zone, but as he backed up, she scuttled back up onto him, gripping tightly with five limbs, though one was now damaged, and directing three punch lasers to one spot. Carapace exploded and ablated away, layers softened with the heat, and she drove her fangs in.

The father-captain's frenzy increased – intelligent enough to know this might kill him. His treads screamed against stone and armour, throwing him across the sanctum and then halfway up one wall. He came off it, over and down, bringing his full weight down on top of her on the floor. She felt some internal struts splintering, but a moment later her fangs broke through into his soft interior. She injected her full load of digestive enzyme at high pressure. The father-captain shrieked as he continued to struggle, flipped back over again, and ran for the doors, crashing into them. Through the gap she could see his children crammed together in one shifting arthropod mass, struggling to bring tools and weapons to bear. He continued shrieking, backed up, mandibles clattering together like mincing blades and spattering half-digested internals being pushed out by reaction pressure inside him. He ran into another wall, then another, and finally collapsed. And Jenny fed.

The pressure build up in the father-captain squirted his dissolving organs and thinning blood inside her. She could see his major ganglion still intact, but detached from portions of his nervous system, and knew he must still be suffering. The feeding was joyous and in every way what she had hoped for. He filled her up in moments and yet still so much more of him remained inside. She retracted her fangs and quickly capped the holes with injections of silk, then staggered back from him under concerted Gatling fire from the doors. Quickly now, using his body as cover, she deployed punch lasers and shears to strip away much of his prosthetics. She then spun silk in cords and attached them all over him before leaping up into her burrow. Weapons fire tracked her, raising more and more damage reports, but in almost drugged ecstasy she hardly noticed as, finally braced above, she heaved him into her burrow, and closed the lid behind her.

It took her some minutes, lubricating his passage with chemically altered silk, to drag him to the slope down through the substance of the base, to the shaft finally dropping towards her cavern. As she reached that, the walls of her burrow broke open behind and prador surged in. With a final nudge she shoved him over and he fell down and down, as she turned her weapons on the pursuers, rail-gunning the first two and thus blocking the entry of those behind. Satisfied with that she dropped down after him scattering silk-decohering beads behind her. At the bottom she looked up to see prador flooding in above, but the wide burrow already collapsing. She dragged him clear as it finally closed and tons of earth and rock dropped down. She had done it!

But the ecstasy began to fade and reality to bite. She understood now that what she had done had in all certainty revealed her presence down here. The prador would come after her. However, right now, they could not. Even with their machines it would take them quite some time to reach her present location. So, Jenny fed again and looked to internal repairs. She planned, in a vague way, to take her prize to another cavern, because she wanted to keep this trophy more than any other.

'Give myself up,' Jenny repeated leadenly, turning now so the majority of her weapons faced towards the area of wall yellow occupied.

'No need to get paranoid,' the AI told her. 'Think about your situation here: you are effectively sealed under the surface of a world. Between you and freedom lies atmosphere – you have to get out of the gravity well. I know you have that capability, but still.'

Jenny inspected herself internally. Yellow's words loosened an easily identifiable psychological block. That she contained a grav engine had been an irrelevance down here. She could also eject high-pressure steam from her spiracles as thrusters, and could create further thrust from most of her weapons. She could fly, but had never needed to, and so had forgotten about it.

'But still,' she prompted, though she began to understand where this was going.

'The moment you get to the surface you'll be targeted and under attack. Quite possibly, deploying chameleonware, you would make it out of atmosphere. But, as you are well aware, that 'ware is power hungry. Thereafter you have to get past the ships and stations around this world, through prador occupied space, then past their border posts.'

'If I decide to head that way.'

'The Graveyard is the most logical destination for you. Whether you then decide to head into the Polity is a decision you will have to face.'

'You are saying such an escape is impossible?'

'It's possible,' Yellow conceded. 'But despite everything Penny Royal installed in you I see no sign of U-space capability. It would take you, flying straight, about a hundred and forty years to get past the border post, then a further eight hundred years to reach an inhabited world, by which time your *human body* would be in hibernation and your power supply depleted to its minimum. I know you can recharge once close enough to a sun, but prior to all this you would have been conscious, drifting through vacuum, for, I estimate, six hundred and thirty years.'

'I could go into hibernation and shut-down early,' said Jenny, wondering why Yellow had placed so much emphasis on *human body*.

'You could, yes, but not until after leaving prador space. If you did it before, your chameleonware would shut down and the prador would sweep you up in an instant. You would have to stay conscious for at least the hundred and forty years ready to react, evade, and use that 'ware when necessary.'

'Give me your calculations,' she said, but distracted now because over on one coast of the continent burrow lids were being opened simultaneously.

The data arrived in her mind and she began processing, while watching the areas around the burrow caps. The same things were happening at each. Overseen in each case by one of the large King's children – now knowing their history and biology she could not say whether they were first- or second-children or if the label even applied any more – local prador had opened the burrow caps. Lined up on the surface by each cap, like newly laid eggs from some immense beast, were spherical war drones. These were smaller than the ones she had encountered before, sported Gatling cannons on each side along with other weapons ports on their bodies. Even as she watched they began to rise from the ground and head towards her burrows.

The data were much as Yellow had said, though limited to a straight escape from the Kingdom. She could see other options, like how she might be able to raid prador bases or ships along the way to resupply. It might also be possible to lose herself in the Kingdom and find another route out. She played with multiple scenarios but, in the end, did not have the time. And she just knew Yellow had been thinking about this for a lot longer, and had a plan.

'They know I can destroy their drones,' she said.

'Of course you can,' Yellow replied. 'But how many and for how long?'

'Of course.' That was the prador strategy then: send these drones against her until she was down to the last dregs of ammo and power, then come and grab her.

'So what is your plan?' she asked.

'Well, when you are finally captured, you will have me with you.'

'Uhuh,' she said, turning towards the exit from the cavern.

'You'll be secured and transported to one of their research bases. The transport of course will be a U-space capable vessel. . .'

'We take it?'

'We do indeed.'

Jenny accelerated with a fierce joy arising inside her. She could see how an awful lot might go wrong with Yellow's plan, but it was a plan at least. She hurtled along one of her burrows, bounced off the wall at one corner while running brief unnecessary diagnostics on her weapons. By now all the drones were down in her system, and there were hundreds of them. Internally she grinned, but then that dropped away and she skidded to a halt. Burrows over that way were winking out of her perception but, from nano-silk along from them she could see what was happening. The last in the lines of drones entering her system had underslung arms and were pausing every now and again to press flat disks against the walls. They were decohering her nano-silk! They were collapsing her burrows behind them as they advanced!

'It seems there is a little more to their strategy,' Yellow observed dryly.

Jenny considered what to do. She wanted to be captured – hopefully with as little damage as possible – but surmised that if she simply gave herself up the prador would be very suspicious and more watchful than if they captured her. In the end her strategy had to be to behave exactly as she would have done two hundred years ago: fight and go down fighting. She accelerated again. On the basis of that strategy, she needed to hit the drones before they completely removed her room to manoeuvre.

Speeding through her burrows she continued to observe them as she headed towards one edge of their incursion. She now noticed a pattern. They were spreading out, seemingly finding the edges of the extent of her burrows to encompass her. This gave her further pause, but a mental one as she continued at speed. It almost looked as if they knew the full extent of her burrows – as if they had a map. Returning her attention to sensors in the burrow caps she observed the prador up there. They had a deal of equipment, especially where shuttles had come down, and some of it was probably scanning gear. But was it likely they now had the technology to penetrate the chameleonware integrated in her nano-silk? She had seen nothing being deployed and sensed nothing in EMR – no X-rays of terahertz scans. Perhaps they had some equipment in those shuttles, or the King's children had it in their armour?

'What are you thinking?' Yellow abruptly asked.

'You don't know?'

'No. While you were a danger to me I maintained my links to your mind, but now I have shut them down. We must trust each other.'

'I am thinking that somehow they have mapped my burrow system. The spread of those drones indicates so.'

'Consider that they have the technology to decohere your nano-silk, and extrapolate.'

Jenny felt a slight surge of annoyance with Yellow. The AI was a bit of a didact. However, the observation was apposite. That the prador could decohere nano-silk meant that they knew what it was, and understood its structure and purpose. She now focused on her own link to the silk throughout her burrows and searched for anomalies. She could find none. The silk still functioned as it should, where linked to opened burrow caps wherever the tunnels below had not been collapsed. . . Then she saw it and transferred her attention to those particular burrow caps the prador had gathered about. They had attached devices to them and the sensor links sat wide open. The fuckers were linking to the nano-silk through her own sensors! She could see no way of stopping this, though the drones might stop it if they collapsed the burrows below those caps, but she suspected the prador would leave some open to maintain their link. They could see where she was as easily as she could see them. And nothing she could do would erase the map they must have by now made of her network. At this she felt a rise in old anger. It was ridiculous really. They had sent down drones after her and these were collapsing her burrows, yet she felt more anger at this *invasion of her privacy*.

The first drone paid for this with a railgun slug straight into the centre of its body. She would have done that anyway, but this time did it with more feeling. She skidded back on the recoil, hooked feet tearing through silk walls, as the drone bounced back in an explosion of incandescent gas, both its Gatling cannons detached and crashing along with it. It slammed into the wall at a turning and sat there smoking, but only briefly. Jenny watched in disbelief as with a whining crunch it pulled itself from the wall, oriented and headed towards her. Its armour was dented to the fore, and a few of those weapons ports were distorted and probably unusable, however, from side ports it dropped two missiles that ignited rocket drives before hitting the floor. Each was only the size of a human finger, but scan return showed them packed with metallised hydrogen. She railed the drone again, straight into where she had hit it before, and had the satisfaction of seeing the exit explosion behind it. The thing just dropped to the floor. Next she flung herself up into the roof of the burrow. The missiles, however, did not sweep on past her, but detonated right below her.

The twin blasts jammed her into the roof, blast waves heading in both directions and the nano-silk turning red hot and losing function. Two of her internal struts broke and other impact damage raised a host of error reports. The struts began to ease back together as she dropped to the floor, laminar shear planes mating up and reintegrating. But of course this all took power. In retrospect she could see this to be the whole purpose of the missiles. They probably would not have hit her directly even if she hadn't moved out of their way. Also in retrospect she realised that if the aim had been to actually kill her, the missiles would have had guidance direct to her body.

She shifted along, tracking the drones all around and seeing all the ones local to her moving into an englobement. Meanwhile the other drones were still on course around the periphery of her network. This indicated that the prador above knew they would not bring her down now so early in the game. She railed the next one twice – her second shot cutting right through its body as before – but still, as it fell smoking out of the air, it released a swarm of missiles from a side port. She ran, calculating fast. Ahead, left tunnel, three more drones coming. She hit the corner hard and rounded it, tearing holes in the wall. The first of the three ahead opened fire with Gatling cannons, another one jamming up beside it to open fire too. She extruded her own cannons and returned fire as she hurtled into them, slamming one into the wall and knocking the other into the one behind. She lashed out with punch lasers and, already having ascertained that their armour was a lot stronger than any she had encountered before, used full power. One she hit issued a high pitched whistling and began spinning like crazy. She delayed moving on past them just long enough for the missiles to arrive and detonate. Even as they exploded she jetted superheated steam from her spiracles, while grabbing the rear drone and shoving it behind her into the pursuing explosion. She hurtled along in then out of the blast.

    Hitting another corner she railed the next drone coming immediately into sight. Just half a second later she opened up with her cannons, filling the burrow with slugs so the missiles it dropped exploded all around it. Mapping positions she headed for the weakest part of the englobement, destroyed four more drones, took a further battering, then decohered the nano-silk behind her. She had the satisfaction of seeing the periphery of collapses encompassing over thirty drones, but had no doubt they could dig themselves out. She now headed for the further edge of their spread about her network, meanwhile assessing her resources. She had plenty of slugs for her railgun and cannons, plenty of metallised hydrogen beads to fire the cannon slugs, and even now her internal manufactories were making more of each. Power was down in laminar storage, but her fusion nodes eating up water and topping it up. A further drain on power was the constant repairs and recycling. Also, if she continued like this, she would need to top up on materials – she would need to feed on metals, composite and organics. It occurred to her, etching out a strategy of attack and retreat, that she might be able to destroy every drone down here. . .

Jenny abruptly slowed, a strange thought arising at variance to her usual thinking. The drones were not just robots, but had once been first- and second-children. They had been living creatures whose ganglions had been installed, through a typically agonising prador process, in drone bodies. She oddly felt a fellow feeling for them, because wasn't she very much like them? Wasn't she a *human body* inside a machine? She slowed even further and then came to a halt. Where was all this coming from? Why the hell after all these years was she starting to feel this . . . guilt? And, as is the way with such self-examination, she found her mind bringing up other exhibits for her inspection: how she had liked to ensure the suffering of her victims by not killing them before injecting the digestive enzymes, those caves full of trophies and, though the count was unclear, how she had killed *thousands*.

'You having a problem over there?' Yellow enquired.

'I thought you had disconnected from my mind,' Jenny spat back.

'I have, but I've noted how you've stopped moving when it seems the best strategy, if you are to maintain the idea that you are evading capture, is to move fast and strike fast.'

'Yes, I have a problem.'

'Perhaps I can be of assistance?'

'Guilt,' she said.

'Ah, that. . .'

'What do you mean by "Ah, that"?'

'I experienced the same when I escaped my container, remembering the people I had killed or left in agony stripped of their skin. One has to understand the shaping process undergone. Penny Royal shaped our bodies and shaped our minds to match its perception of what we should be in those bodies. But Penny Royal, in removing itself from present existence, removed that imposed template. The underlying mind reverts to an earlier state.'

'I see . . . but I have the spider in me. . .'

'Yes, I saw some traces of arachnid neural function – previously maintained at high strength but now subjugated and being absorbed by the much stronger and more complex human mind. You are remembering who you are, Jenny Kelland.'

'Who I am?' she said, but could say no more because she had delayed too long.

Drones began to appear. Automatically she fired on them but not the double railgun shots that destroyed them. Missiles came seeking her and she rapidly retreated, scattering decohering beads as she went. She sped up a pipe, wanting to head towards the centre of her network to just hide, and contemplate, but instead heading towards another group of drones. She engaged, retreated, engaged again. She wasn't fighting strategically but chaotically. Her heart was no longer in this and she just wanted it to be over. Data from her nano-silk showed her drones now all across one side of her network and advancing, collapsing the burrows behind them. She darted from group to group, using up her ammo and depleting her power to little practical effect. Perhaps the prador above would think she had just panicked, or malfunctioned. Next noting drones moving down deep and collapsing burrows faster than to the side, she could now see that their strategy, as well as getting her to deplete herself against them, was to drive her to the surface. Something awaited there, and she wanted to find out what it was now.

Pulling out of yet another fight where she left drones damaged and fleeing in a firestorm of explosions, she entered another pipe and headed upwards. She paused briefly at one of her caverns to gaze in at the mounded prador armour. To human perception the prador were monsters of the worst sort who delighted in the agony and the destruction of anything that was not them. They also delighted in the same for competitors of their own kind, including their own kin, their own children. But now she had a moment of epiphany, understanding that here on this world, she was the monster. Suddenly, on impulse, she opened up with all her weapons on the mound, firing her railgun until its rails turned red hot in her body, Depleting her cannon slugs, draining power through lasers, firing metallised hydrogen into the mass. As this firestorm drove her back and the cavern roof collapsed, it just seemed a right and proper expression of madness, but she knew nothing she could do could wipe out her past.

Jenny turned away and entered another pipe, used power to eject superheated steam and shot up to the cap at the top with her legs folded against her body. She hit the cap hard and then exploded through a two-metre layer of soil. In an incredibly bright day she engaged her grav engine for the first time, fifty feet above the ground, and stretched out her legs. All around her in the sky she could see thrusters flames from prador armour and from numerous shuttles shaped like the carapaces of horseshoe crabs. The air hazed and from every direction BIC vortex lasers locked onto her, raising informational warfare by induction over her skin, disrupting her systems. Grav just went out and she started to fall. By instinct she fought the incursions but, again, without the appetite to win. She saw missiles coming in at high speed after the beam strikes and wondered, briefly, if actually they were trying to destroy her. But the missiles split and broke open, flinging out square mesh sheets that hit her hard and wrapped round her. She hit the ground amidst boulders, almost completely enclosed in this tangle of braided monofilament nets and it seemed somehow appropriate that she, a giant mechanical spider, had been captured this way.

Giving some evidence of attempting to escape she struggled against the nets as the prador descended, tried to cut her way out with punch lasers, tried to hit the prador with her few remaining munitions. Two prador, smaller than the others and loaded with tools, their armour pure polished chrome, moved in. From what at first looked like weapons attached to their claws they sprayed jets of a substance that boiled and bubbled up amidst the nets all around her, expanding and hardening into a tough meta-material close-cell foam. And finally she was completely trapped. She could gaze out of her trap with her full spectrum EMR senses, but chose not to, closing them down and settling into the darkness.

When the prador entered her burrows she delighted in their presence. She did not have to go in search of her prey anymore because it was coming to her. They tried to establish a grid search pattern but were obviously blind down here, while she could see them distinctly. She first took those who strayed too far from their fellows and replete after feeding on four of them, wondered what to do about her next victims. She decided on a new approach, disabling them with accurate underpower railgun shots, then rushing in deploying hardfields to then engage close and destroy their limbs with punch lasers. These immobilized but still living prey she dragged off to her various caverns.

This approach did not last long as they pulled together and searched in groups of no less than five. She retreated and considered the problem, then reluctantly decided some would have to die quickly. The first group she attacked she railgunned at full power, the shots punching through and spraying flaming chunks of prador up the walls, and in one case the impact so hard it flipped up the upper lid of one suit. Three she killed like that, remembering her times of starvation and feeling a stab of regret at such waste. The two remaining she advanced on with hardfields ahead. When finally close enough she blinked the hardfields, activating them like shears to snip of limbs, then went in close again with punch lasers. She was about to drag the two off but had to abandon them when another group approached rapidly. This alerted her to how they were establishing communication nodes in her burrows.

The next group she just killed, quickly and with extreme force, and moved on to the next. She simply could not allow this incursion to continue. She then mapped out positions and deployed a new strategy, annoyed that she had not thought of it before. She began herding them and deploying decohering beads, timing things just right to collapse burrows and trap many of them. Finally, the force went into retreat, departing through her burrow caps. She watched and waited for some days, but they did not return, so she went to dig up those she had buried, strip off their legs and secure them in her caverns. She now had, she estimated, enough of them to last her for . . . well, for as long as she needed.

Feeding on her captured prey she started to feel bored and realised that a deal of the satisfaction she garnered wasn't just from the kill, but from the hunt. She kept heading towards the surface, then changing her mind and going back down again. It just seemed wasteful to go hunting again, while her larder was stocked. She worked her way through her stock of limbless prador, eating one every few days, but after eight of them she had almost persuaded herself to go hunting again. Surely it was a good idea to keep in practise, and surely it was a good idea to grab prador from the surface while they were plentiful? The prador presence on this world might be put to an end at any time. . .

She felt gratitude when one of her burrow caps activated because it had been opened. She sped for the surface assessing what the cap sensors and nano-silk below were showing her. Prador had gathered there and, while she watched, they dropped an object down into the burrow. She paused, tracking its long fall to a bottom-point crossroads, then bouncing unnaturally along one of the transverse burrows. Closer inspection revealed a two-limbed robot hopping like a flea. It found its way to another shaft and dropped down lower. Watching its progress she could see it was following a simple program to find the lowest point it could. In fact, though simple, the program did get it almost to her lowest burrows, where it exploded.

The blast wasn't major nor was it hot, but it lasted a long time producing a cloud of gas. This progressed unusually fast, and spread out through her burrows. She surmised specially-designed reactive dispersants. Understanding where such things were used she set nano-silk to analysing the gas. It didn't take long, and the results puzzled her. They had deployed a potent nerve-gas that could kill a wide variety of life forms. It seemed a stupid tactic because surely by now they realised she was a machine?

Moving through her burrows she entered one of her storage caverns and scanning the prador hoarded there found that they had died. This annoyed her, because dead prador soon decayed and became unpalatable. She grabbed one of them and pulled it towards her. At least she could feed on perhaps two or three of these before that happened. She had just started to drive her fangs into this first one, when mad panic surged through her. Pulling her fangs free she bounced back, hurling the prador from her. How had she forgotten that inside, in that compartment inside, she was human? Had she fed on this prador she would have taken the toxins straight inside. Now she began assessing her defences, raising systems never used before, to track that nerve gas. It had entered her spiracles, her spinnerets, had progressed some way up her fangs too. It had entered limp joints and between her body segments.

Having already analysed its chemistry she used the same newly-initiated system to make a counteragent and begin dispersing it inside her. She then, with a massive effort of will tried to focus on her core, on her vulnerable core. Here she found layers of protections and scanning forward saw that the gas would not have gotten as far as her semi-human intestines before being ejected. She checked the slow trickle of oxygen supply yet, alerted to the danger, her system had switched over to supplying it from the cracking of water. And finally, fighting a long established block she focused on that core. It kept sliding in and out of perception but now, for the first time in years, she saw the effect of her steady feeding. Within the body mould lay a skinless thing, nested in clear gel. Why she had perceived something bloody before she had no idea, for it was bloodless grey and white, almost like a Da Vinci anatomical drawing. It was healthy, alive, and none of the poison had penetrated. She found herself locked in contemplation of it, hypnotised by it, yet unable to think about it in any meaningful manner. But then, an alert through her nano-silk pulled her attention away, and she found herself gladly retreating from this internal inspection, feeling somehow dirty.

Prador had entered through burrow caps – just four of them. She began to head up to meet them, considering her strategy. Her burrows were flooded with nerve gas so she could not feed on them since that would let it into their armour. She also could not capture them by stripping away their legs, because that would open their suits too. She would just have to kill them. They had entered through widely-separated burrows, so she chose the nearest and headed towards it. But then she paused.

Obviously they had understood that, though she might appear to be a machine like the Polity drones that had attacked here, she did have organic components that needed to be fed. They had seen that feeding. They had seen the remains. It probably made perfect sense to them – since their own war machines were run by the ganglions of their own kind. Hence the deployment of that nerve gas, and hence this limited number of sacrificial searchers to find out if she was dead, since prador father-captains were rather careless of their children's lives. So maybe it would be better to hide and let them think they had killed her – that she had disappeared into some deep place to die? She could return once they finished their search. She could run deactivation chem through the nano-silk to be rid of the last of the nerve gas, though that might not be necessary since its chemistry was such that it would break down quickly.

No.

Such a move would have been entirely logical, but she had long understood that complex and well built as she was, she did not run on the logic of an AI. She would kill these interlopers fast. She would kill any others that came down here. Yes, she would be rid off the nerve gas and then, she would return to feeding.

She watched the prador – it was a second-child – making its way down into her burrows. It seemed to be moving quite clumsily and kept bouncing off the walls. Was it frightened? Almost certainly it was, but usually that did not interfere with their physical control. She drew closer and closer, onlined a railgun shot then paused to check integrity around the weapon, not wanting to let nerve gas inside by using it. All was good as she rounded the last corner and brought the creature in sight. Here she paused, noting it did not possess Gatling cannons or any carapace-mounted weaponry, nor did it drop the tip of one claw to expose a particle cannon. The thing just kept coming towards her, neither accelerating nor slowing down.

Something was wrong.

Jenny scanned into the thing, briefly wondering if either nerve gas had penetrated its suit or those above had deliberately presented her with prey poisoned in another way. But inside the suit she found no prador at all. The suit was being remotely controlled. And inside it sat a cylinder packed with tech and wedges of explosive around a sphere of plutonium with a hollow core. She recognised an atomic bomb, and further processing that had not been part of her human mind, added the identification of a neutron bomb. She turned and ran, firing superheated steam from her spiracles, hit a shaft top, smashing into the wall hard enough to shatter struts, jetted and ran down, legs cracking as they passed the speed of sound here. Hundreds of metres of her burrows around the prador suit just disappeared from her perception. The pulse of radiation hit her as she hit the shaft bottom. Immediately, from every part of her body the error reports arose, then disrupted and minced together in her mind. She could feel things failing as she ran along from the bottom of that shaft heading for another that went way down, and found herself crashing against the walls like the badly-controlled suit above.

Systems simply began disappearing within her as a fiery blast wave pursued her down then mauled her along the burrow. This assisted her into the next shaft, where she simply fell. Burning nano-silk above gave her a hint of burrows collapsing, but whether it was dying under the radioactive assault or her receivers were, she did not know, but the signal disappeared. The fall seemed to last forever, and an instant, as her perception of time died. She hit a mound of broken slate scattered with the dismembered remains of prador armour, bounced down this and landed in an underground river, raising a cloud of steam from her near red hot body. Things cracked with the sudden cooling – so much died – but two limbs and some perception of her surroundings persisted, and some survival instinct too. Washed along in the flow she managed to briefly access a map of her locality. As quickly as she could, she propelled herself to one side of the flow and, at the right point, reached out and snared a gut-like mass of travertine and swung round it, straight into a side cavern gnawed out by the river as, over the ages, it had shifted course underground. Her senses were dying now and her surroundings unclear, also blurred by the silt she stirred up. She settled to the bottom and with one last effort jammed her moveable limbs into a long crack. She considered the likelihood of her soft core having been killed by the radiation pulse, but not for long, for her mind just went out.

'Jenny . . . Jenny!'

The voice was an irritation, because it did not fit. How could anyone be talking to her deep underground in this water-filled cavern? She tried to move her limbs, but obviously they were still malfunctioning from the neutron blast. She tried to focus on the two that had been moveable, which she had jammed into the crack, but she could not move them either. Only belatedly did she snap out of it and realise the cavern lay in her past, and remember she was tangled in mesh, sunk in hard foam, and a captive of the prador.

'That informational warfare was good,' she said. 'AI level stuff.'

'Meaning?' Yellow enquired.

'I lost myself, sank into delusion. I shut down my senses and now cannot bring them back online. I am in darkness.'

'Well, the prador still have their detestation of AI, but they seized a great deal of technology during the war, and now buy it too across the Graveyard.'

'Presumably not from the AIs?'

'If there's money to be made there are always those who fail to question the morality of their trade. Some humans in the Graveyard are even now selling cored and thralled humans to the prador.'

'And the Polity allows this?'

'The Graveyard is effectively the Wild West.'

'Still. . .'

'Polity agents do take down numerous operations, but more spring up, while some are quite strong and well defended. The truce does not allow Kingdom or Polity military presence there. As for the technology, many of those who sell it convince themselves it will drive the prador towards adopting AI which will civilize them. They never met Penny Royal.'

The conversation was a rolling distraction as Jenny directed her concentration internally. Her model of her system was of a constellation of lights, blinking on and off out of phase with each other. Her perception now sank below that, straying away from the human sensorium and into the AI realms of code, mathematical constructs, information time crystals and other suitably obscure functions. She began finding the points of disruption and repairing them, the nests of viruses and vores and erasing them, the columns of data flow and bringing them back into phase. Her balance and sense of position came back first, and she realised she was being moved.

'Do you need any help in there?' Yellow asked. 'I can reconnect if you like.'

'That will not be necessary,' she replied. 'Describe the situation out there for me.'

'I could send you visuals. . .'

'Which will disrupt what I am now doing. Tell me.'

'Well, you're on a grav sled and being taken towards a prador reaver down on the surface. I didn't even know the things could land. Impressive sight.'

More of her began to come online. The ability to move her limbs restored abruptly, but she found little movement available – just a slight ability to flex against the enclosing foam. She flexed and continued to flex for a little while, thinking in terms of escape, then shut that down when her diagnostic feed came up and alerted her to just how little power she had available.

'These prador are taking you very seriously, by the way.'

'In what sense?'

'In that they are all around with weapons locked and loaded. Their particle beamers are all uncapped too. And they sank an EMP into that foam enclosing you.'

'I see.' She was distracted again, pursuing the power problems. Her fusion nodes had all simply stopped and she was running on the dregs in laminar storage. Focusing on one node she found the virally implanted instruction to shut it down and deleted it, but then it just reappeared copied from other nodes in the network. She isolated the node and tried again. This time the shutdown instruction stayed away. Focusing on another nodes she began to design a virus of her own to simultaneously erase all the shutdown instructions, but then saw that doing so would raise an overpower instruction that would burn out her laminar storage. With an internal AI sigh she went back to dealing with each node individually – all one hundred and twelve of them.

'Interesting stuff,' said Yellow.

'What is?' Jenny asked, feeling a stab of irritation.

'The foam entrapping you. It's based on spaceship crash foam – breach sealant – but contains a semi-decoherer for monofilament. I guess you can't see but the nets they hit you with initially are all but gone. The foam broke them up into short threads it incorporated as it hardened, rendering it very tough indeed.'

'More Polity technology?'

'No, this is prador stuff. It's always well to remember that it wasn't just their metallurgy that was way ahead of the Polity when they attacked, but all their materials science.'

'Yet they did that without AI.'

Yes, Yellow irritated her occasionally, but the conversation kept her from losing herself like one of those Polity AIs that, while studying, sank into terminal navel-gazing. It helped specifically because her time sense was wonky again – it allowed her to keep it sort of on track.

'They created an interstellar civilization. I think the Polity AIs, calling it a kingdom, were being deliberately disparaging.'

With the last fusion node up and running, Jenny carefully reconnected their network, hoping she had missed nothing. It was good – the nodes feeding power into her laminar storage but also into the rest of her system. This kicked online repairs both physical and mental, and within just a few seconds her world exploded with light. Nanites within began sealing up cracks and remoulding damaged meta-materials, larger robots and robot systems worked on larger repairs. She delighted in her internal perception of her functions ramping up, but still evaded looking closely at that soft core. She knew she would have to at some point and wondered now if she would find a corpse. Surely, if the neutron bomb had not killed that human body, two hundred years of shutdown must have? She wondered if she resided wholly in the scattered AI crystal and other processing substrates.

Her senses powered up and now she looked through the foam around her, briefly inspecting the EMP sitting close by, then ranging out. The grav sled was sliding along above a plain of dusty red scattered with wind and weather rounded slabs. Between these the black and white sprouts of some plant, or perhaps animal, stuck up from the ground like thorns. All around were prador, all as large as first-children, some walking, many sliding through the air on grav engines. They were a colourful host indeed with armour patterned with swirls, chequers, Euclidian shapes, Rorschach blots and other more imaginative designs. It still baffled her to see such artistic expression from prador. Behind the sled walked the two in chromed armour. They now had large wide-barrelled weapons mounted on their backs and, briefly running a scan over these, she saw they were vortex lasers similar to those that had brought her down but, judging by the size of the power supplies and the fifteen laser inputs into the magneto-electrostatic barrels, were probably capable of punching holes through her armour. Yes, they were taking her seriously.

Ahead, now just a kilometre away, lay the reaver and, as Yellow had said, it was impressive. The extended teardrop gleamed red gold in the dawn. It had its protrusions of weapons, sensors and other paraphernalia, but they all smoothly integrated into the whole. She saw prador in the air around it like bees from a hive, open airlocks in the hull, and a large entrance lying ahead with a ramp down on the red dirt.

'So we take control of that?' said Jenny, now utterly sure there was no possibility of that happening. That was one massive ship and she counted in an instant over three hundred prador around her and around it.

'Maybe there will be other options,' said Yellow.

'Other options,' she repeated leadenly. 'Where are you, Yellow Azimuth?'

'Maybe you can work out who the boss prador is here – the captain of that ship?'

Jenny scanned and tried to tune into prador chatter. The talk was coded and she found it very difficult to penetrate, however she could track the pattern of it and found most issuing from a prador drifting along above her. She looked at this creature. Spirals with a Celtic look patterned its armour, but only when she translated her EMR view of it to the human spectrum did she see that the spirals were bright yellow.

'The leader has yellow armour,' she said, feeling a horrible suspicion. 'How convenient for you.'

'Now don't start getting paranoid again. The paint on this armour can be set to any colour. I introduced a fault when I occupied it that Captain Vottle has not been inclined to correct. Perhaps he likes my shade.'

'Okay,' said Jenny, but no more as she inspected the comlink now insistently banging against her system. It was tight beam high-frequency radio and she tracked it back to that drifting *yellow* prador. It obviously wasn't from Yellow Azimuth, so it seemed this Captain Vottle wanted to speak to her. Since she was their prisoner, and could be taken down by vortex lasers or that EMP at any time, she did not worry about informational warfare through the link, so allowed it.

'We perceive that you are conscious again,' said the prador, speaking perfect Anglic. 'I do hope that your sensors are working well enough for you to understand your situation.'

'I understand my situation very well,' she replied, meanwhile using those same sensors to closely examine the foam trapping her. It was as Yellow had described: similar to crash foam but now with threads of monofilament incorporated. It would be almost impossible for her to break it because it would merely deform and then, via the tension in those threads, regain its form.

'If you attempt to escape you will be further immobilised. We do not wish to use the EMP, since so close to you it will kill your organic components and erase a great deal of data, but we will if you become a danger.'

'I'm not really sure why you are stating the obvious,' she said.

She contemplated using her lasers on the foam. Now beginning to get its chemical profile saw that it would melt and thus she could escape it. But then she got readings from the monofilament threads and saw that they were highly conductive, in fact edging towards being superconductors. Making further calculations she saw that they would draw off and distribute the laser heat and, even using all her lasers, it would take her a good twenty minutes to melt the mass sufficiently for escape. But there had to be something else, for the prador would want access to her, so must have a way of removing this stuff.

'I opened conversation with you in a typically threatening prador manner,' said Vottle. 'It feels like some traditions must be adhered to.'

That gave her sudden pause. The supposed threat had seemed like just cautionary instruction and to a degree unpradorish. From what she had listened in on during their fight with the Polity, they usually started out describing the nasty things they intended to do to their victims. And now this? She understood that these king's children were very different indeed.

'Opened conversation to what purpose?' she asked.

The chemical profile of the foam continued to grow – the model of it propagating in her mind. The lengthy molecular chains were characteristic of DNA, and soon she found its version of a telomere. And there she saw it, because in some sense it was very much like her nano-silk. The lock was there, and this foam had a key somewhere. It could be decohered.

'It is our intention to learn as much as possible from you. Throughout the entire war with the Polity, we only managed to capture a total of twenty-eight drones intact, and of them only seven were from Room 101. During their deconstruction we learned a great deal from them.'

'And so you want to learn from me?'

She focused her attention on those parts of her that fashioned the beads to decohere nano-silk, copied across the foam's molecular make up and began constructing a key. Maybe it was something she would not use to escape at once, but a good idea to have it ready.

'There is much to learn,' said Vottle. 'When we thought you destroyed by the neutron bomb we were under the impression that you were just another Polity drone gone rogue. Only recently have we learned that you were directly constructed by the Dark Intelligence.'

Jenny puzzled over that. The prador's Anglic was perfect and the choice of those words to describe Penny Royal must have been deliberate. It implied respect and fear. Perhaps in the end this was understandable since Penny Royal had performed its transformations on prador too, and she had no doubt they knew about the AI's apotheosis.

'Indeed I was,' she replied.

They reached the ramp going up into the ship and there the sled paused while numerous prador shot in ahead. Scanning inside she found a lot of meta-material blocking, but she could divine the shape of the interior. The prador going in ahead were positioning themselves in side-corridors along a route winding in towards a chamber that had masses of equipment packed in around it.

'I hope you're coming up with a plan,' she said to Yellow.

'I'm working it out,' the paint AI replied. 'I am perfectly positioned to seize control of Vottle, and thus the other prador and the ship itself.'

That seemed perfectly plausible, but Jenny was starting to get some serious doubts about all this. Yellow had assumed she would be transported elsewhere for examination yet, judging by the equipment around that chamber, it seemed likely the examination was to be conducted aboard this vessel. She felt that once she arrived in that chamber she would reach a point of no return. How much did she trust Yellow Azimuth? More than she should since she felt sure the AI had lied to her either directly or by omission on occasion. After a pause of five minutes the sled began to proceed up the ramp, the two chrome prador behind and Vottle settling to the ramp to walk in behind them.

'Perhaps you would like to talk about your history?' Vottle suggested.

'Why are you under the impression that I will cooperate with you?' Jenny asked.

'Because you are a rational being, perhaps?'

'As a rational being I'm thoroughly aware of how the prador treat other rational beings.'

'We are different,' he said.

The comment raised curiosity. Until now she had simply accepted Yellow's explanation of the king's children and looked no further than the designs on their armour. Now she probed back towards Vottle, incidentally also to see if Yellow might be active in some way – perhaps penetrating the prador's armour systems. She used active scan, since there was no point now passively gathering data. As with areas of the ship, meta-materials in the armour resisted penetration. She could see the nano-scopic complexity of Yellow in those spirals but otherwise it seemed inert. She pushed along the spectrum available to her, which was limited by the enclosing foam and those highly conductive threads. Flashes of structure came back to her but she could not get a full picture before the meta-material disrupted signal and she had to change frequencies. She would have loved to have put a vortex laser on that armour to get a read, but unfortunately that was just not possible. Instead she began weaving those fragments of imagery into a whole. It turned out to be a whole very little like *natural* prador.

Vottle was as fibrous as those human blanks she and the drone had burned, but unlike them his overall shape had been changed. The head turret, she saw, had flattened and jutted forwards, the mandibles were now quite similar to her chelicerae while the eyes had shifted. Vottle had two large binocular eyes to the fore, subsidiary eyes down the sides of his head and had lost his eye stalks. She also ascertained that the head turret had become a full head, and sat down close to the body over the loop of a long muscular neck. He still had the same number of limbs and they looked quite standard, but his body was now ribbed, long and louse like, coiled in at the back to fit into armour the wrong shape for it. This then was why the king's children all looked the size of first-children – they needed the larger armour to accommodate their highly mutated forms. From this need for concealment she surmised that other prador might not react well upon seeing it, and now she understood the meta-material shielding in the armour.

'Have you had enough of a look?' Vottle enquired.

'Yes, I think so.' A second later the meta-materials in the armour became more active, completely blocking her. She realised he had allowed her to see. 'You're very different physically, but that does not necessarily make you trustworthy.'

The sled had entered the ship now and, meanwhile, Jenny finally had a decoder for the foam enclosing her and began manufacturing it fast – lining it up to be squirted from her spiracles. She felt great urgency now because the deeper she got into that ship, the fewer options she would have left available.

'Consider straight-forward self-interest,' said Vottle. 'We want to learn as much from you as possible, because the technology of the Dark Intelligence even from over two hundred years ago is still in advance of the Polity. With your cooperation we can learn a great deal more than we would by simply killing and dismantling you.'

'Why should I help you kill my own kind?'

'So you acknowledge what you were. . .'

'Yes, I was human and you killed my kind. You have slaughtered many people! Why should I help you get the power to kill more?'

'We do not now seek weapons to destroy the Polity, merely some degree of parity. We seek some degree of power, of defence, of leverage, to make it too costly for the AIs should they at decide to exterminate us. We know that without our own AI, we stand little chance against the Polity now.'

'And I am supposed to believe that?' Jenny asked. 'And am I supposed to be concerned about the AIs making such a decision, which I am certain they would not?'

'You hate us,' said Vottle.

Jenny fell silent. She had just been asking rote questions and giving rote replies, but she understood that no, she did not hate the prador. In fact, directly after Penny Royal inserted her in this spider body she had no hate, just the need to feed. Thinking back she realised that her losses had never been given a chance to develop into hate.

'Do you know how many of us you have killed?' Vottle asked.

Her systems had pretty much restored after she came out of that watery cavern. Now, trapped in this foam, recent damage was healing up. But nothing could restore memories that had been erased by the radiation pulse. She had an impression of numerous kills and of course there were those caverns filled with prador armour. But she also had a recollection of changing her system of burrows, of occasionally collapsing caverns to create new ones above, or burrowing to find new ones.

'Not really,' she said.

'Neither do we. When we penetrated your nano-silk we managed to make a bit of a count, but were soon aware that the structure of your network had been changed many times during the forty-eight solstan years you hunted us.'

'Forty-eight years?' Jenny repeated. That simply made no sense – the creature was delusional surely? A great unease crept over her as she started to sense that Vottle might be telling her the truth.

'Out best estimate comes from a statistical analysis of the prador who disappeared here. We know that some were lost in accidents or to local life forms, but in those cases it was rare for some remains, or the armour not to be recovered. Rounding up we think you killed over eight thousand prador.'

'Nonsense,' Jenny spat. 'Why are you saying these things?'

The conversation was a constant distraction and she quickly focused back on immediate problems. She was in the ship now and heading down towards that chamber. Deeper in and she could get a closer look. The thing was spherical with all around ram-driven heads that could enter to a central point. A brief examination of one of these showed it loaded with tools ranging from the nano to the macroscopic, complex scanners, manipulators and, inevitably, cutting gear.

'Yellow,' she said urgently to the paint AI. 'This is not looking good at all. What are you doing? How are we to deal with this?'

'You know,' said Yellow contemplatively. 'I think Vottle underestimated the number. I did my own count down there and my own projections and put the figure above eleven thousand. I reckon some of the father-captains that came here, or came through here, under-reported their losses.'

'What?' said Jenny, baffled by the response.

'Just be patient – everything is under control,' said Yellow.

'Patient!'

'I am slowly and carefully penetrating the computing in this suit,' said Yellow. 'It is a complicated task, but the suit contains programs just like any other prador suit to run it should the occupant be dead. Once I have that it will be easy enough to then copy Vottle's communications.'

'How long will this take you?'

'Maybe a couple of hours.'

The sled had progressed quickly into the ship and now that chamber loomed ahead. Yellow told her to be patient but only after rambling about the prador Jenny had killed. She just knew something was not as it should be as the sled entered that chamber and settled to the floor. The two chromed prador came in and moved round it. Vottle came in and drifted up high on grav. Grabs came in from the walls, severing the straps holding the mass of hardened foam, and her, down on the sled and closed long metal fingers about the mass. They picked it up and began transferring it towards a thick column in the centre of the floor, shaped in its upper surface. She saw a hollow there in the shape of her abdomen and cephalothorax. She did not know what that meant and found, finally, she did not trust Yellow, and began ejecting the decoder from her spiracles. One of the chromed prador came up beside her and sprayed something about the EMP from a device on one claw. The foam there decohered and it lifted the EMP out and backed away.

The decoherence from the EMP continued as grabs lowered the mass into the recess in the top of that column, while above she saw another column descending. The foam directly around her began to decohere from her own chemical key and she became able to shift some of her body mounted weapons. She trained lasers on the two chromed prador and loaded up a shot to her railgun, though the only possible target at the moment was the open doorway into here. She began to flex her limbs preparing to abruptly shed the softening foam, stripping and burning it away with her punch lasers.

'Too late,' Vottle informed her.

The upper column shrieked down, explosively driven by hydraulics above. A brief scan had revealed the columns above and below to be the kind of exotic alloy prador used in their ship hulls. She tried to fling herself clear, now seeing the wedge-shaped blades above that would mate in recesses below, but the foam just had not yet softened enough. She fired all her lasers, fired up her punch lasers too to try and strip it away. The upper column hit the decohering foam, pressing it away explosively. The whole thing was like a giant cold forge press. Her body slammed down, turning and sliding to perfectly fit the form below. The upper shaped surface closed in above, throwing out every last trace of the foam as it fitting over her exactly with a resonant crash. Her punch lasers went out, all feedback from her legs disappeared. Her head lay clear of the press and she could see just about everything, except right behind where the column sat. She saw all her legs clattering to the floor.

'We calculated that you would make a decoder,' said Vottle. 'Fortunately you delayed long enough before using it and there was no necessity to use the EMP to immobilise you – it would cause damage we did not want.' He then added, 'We would have preferred not to remove your legs, since that has damaged some intricate technology, but it is best to be cautious around killing machines such as you.'

She noted heat spikes on her armour – extreme almost to fusion level and enough to burn through it, but saw that her body was being welded into place in the lower column. The heat shifted steadily around her, then appeared in other spots, filling up the laser pores on her body, tracing the outlines of the hatches over her cannons. She continued to gaze at her legs and now found the situation oddly hilarious. Even as the welding completed the upper column began to rise. All her weapons, but for her railgun had been negated, and even that had a chunk of the column metal right in front of it. She did not think it a good idea to fire the weapon. Firstly she had no target and nothing to gain by doing so, secondly, the railgun shot would probably turn into a lethal plasma ricochet off that metal, burn out the gun and blast back inside her.

'And now,' said Vottle, 'it is time to remove the other impediment to our work.'

EMR flashed from the meta-materials in his amour – a scream across the spectrum loaded with viruses and vores. It blinded her, turning the prador into a small sun. Through her link to Yellow she heard the paint AI scream. The flash began to fade and she saw Vottle now spinning in midair on thrusters, the spirals on his armour shifting. Abruptly a sheet like old dead skin slewed away, hit one wall and stuck. It paused there bubbling as the two chromed prador fired up their vortex beam and began to scour it. She saw Yellow burning and heard a fading wail, but she also watched the remainder of the AI slide down the wall and sink through an air vent. So that was it.

'Hunt it down,' Vottle clattered, and she understood enough of prador speech to read his irritation. That could maybe have given her hope, because obviously the intent had been to destroy Yellow here, but she had none. These prador had demonstrated their superiority in every way, had anticipated every move and had known about Yellow. As if to hammer the point home, as the two chromed prador departed, two others in baroque red and yellow armour came in to collect up her legs and take them away.

Vottle settled down to hover in front and to one side of her, perhaps anticipating that she might try to fire her railgun. 'Your deconstruction will began once we are clear of this world and a little further away from the border.' He turned and went out through the doors, and they ground closed behind him.

Oddly, Jenny found the powerlessness comforting. For decade upon decade she had spent her time constantly in action, plotting the next kills, altering her burrows, making her kills and subsequently concealing traces. Now, the absolute finality of her capture left her without anything to plan and anything to do . . . it was almost relaxing. Another stray thought arrived on top of this feeling. Maybe it would be good to be deconstructed and for everything that she was to finally come to an end?

She sat there stuck on the column contemplating that, playing with the thought and analysing it from different angles. She understood it arose out of a loss of purpose and some degree of guilt. Vengeance in the end could not be eternal. The race that had attacked the Polity and destroyed her previous life was no longer at war and she had killed thousands of its members. And, in the end, she had lost her appetite for the kill. However, when she felt the reaver shift and expanded her scanning outwards, introspection waned and she took more interest in the activity around her. She could feel the tug of grav engines and sense enough through internal meta-material shielding to know the ship had risen from the planet's surface to head for vacuum.

Drawing her attention back in closer she searched for and found her legs – they came clearer to her senses than much else here. The two prador who had taken them had mounted them in complex gimbals – one for each leg – that had numerous instruments affixed. They were scanning them down to nanoscopic levels and carefully, meticulously disassembling them. Just as an experiment, she sent a nerve impulse signal to one point of severance and saw one of the legs flex in its frame. This confirmed that the nerve impulses, which could cross any break in the system caused by battle damage, could cross a much wider gap. The moving leg drove the prador into frenzied almost panicked activity as they checked the security of clamps. She also noted how they next carefully put some shielding around the feet, just in case the punch lasers fired up. She acknowledged now that she could fire them from here, but saw no advantage in doing so.

Scanning further she found one of the chromed prador squatting by an air vent. It had a case open beside it in which things moved, but she couldn't quite see what they were until it took one out. Then she saw a ship louse – one of the arthropods the prador encouraged in their ships to clean up debris. It looked a bit like a trilobite but now she saw further differences. The chitin segments of its carapace alternated with ones of polished metal and other devices were attached. It seemed that the prador love of technologically enslaving living creatures now extended to these. While she watched, the prador inserted the louse into the air vent. It scuttled off into the darkness. The prador put the grating back, then closed the case and moved on. She had no doubt that these things were programmed to hunt down what remained of Yellow.

She mentally meandered through the interior of the ship she could see, starting to get bored with it, until she saw the woman. That startled her and focused her attention. What the hell was a human doing aboard? The woman wore a grey reinforced overall and heavy boots. She was bald and heavily built but, it was only when Jenny translated her scanning to human range did she see that her skin had the hue of one who had been drowned, and was covered with circular blue scars. Focusing harder she detected the fibrous constituency within. Here walked a human blank like those she and the drone had destroyed long ago in her tunnels. Jenny's focus blurred, moved away.

As the activity around her ceased to hold her interest, she returned to thinking about her situation. She now did begin to explore the possibility of escape, but just as an intellectual exercise. Yes, she had been welded to a column, her legs removed and all her weapons but her railgun effectively shut down. However, if she could somehow free herself, she did have her grav engine and she could still steer using planing of that engine and superheated steam from her spiracles as jets. So what could she do? They had not removed her fangs and she could still move her hinged chelicerae. She hinged those out, extruded her fangs and brought them down on that lump of metal sitting in front of her railgun, and started up the chain-diamond cutter. Half an hour later she retracted them, noting a few scratches on the surface of the metal and a need to manufacture more diamond threads inside. It was hopeless.

'Well that was unexpected,' said a voice.

'Rumours of your demise were exaggerated,' she replied, then tried to trace from where the silly phrase had originated. Oh yes, some joke from Gogh, back when she had been human.

'Difficult to wipe out a distributed system like me,' Yellow replied. 'I constantly copy across and the essential me exists in thousands of quantum crystal conglomerations throughout. I did lose a lot of substance and am now rebuilding. An interesting ship louse just provided some of the materials.'

'You're sounding chipper, but then you aren't sans legs and welded to a column waiting to be disassembled.'

'The greatest blow has been to my ego,' Yellow replied dryly.

'It doesn't matter,' said Jenny impatiently. 'We failed and that's the end to it. They've started taking me apart and will continue, I'll die, and in the end it doesn't matter.'

'You're depressed.'

'No, just realistic.'

'No, not realistic because they're not taking you apart, at least, not yet.'

She sent an image link to the paint AI of the prador pulling apart her legs.

'Yes, I saw that,' said Yellow, 'but that's not you.'

'What?'

'This vessel has a fast picket attached that is capable of U-space travel. I am currently occupying a decal on its hull and checking things out. I'll probably be able to undo the docking clamps from within the picket, but I'm thinking on cutting those clamps anyway just to be sure – thankfully they're not an exotic alloy like that column you're attached to.'

'What are you talking about?'

Oblivious to the question, Yellow continued, 'Did you notice the blanks?'

'Yes, I saw one.'

'There are a few hundred aboard, going round doing maintenance like the Polity uses robots. The king won't risk antagonising the Polity by buying any of those newly cored and thralled from the Graveyard but has no objection to continuing with those from the war.'

'I would have thought most dead by now.'

'No, the exceptional ruggedness the Spatterjay virus imparts, roots deep into the genome – blanks are practically immortal.'

She accepted that and could see some horror in it. She could also see the king's point of view. The blanks were mindless – no more than biological mechanisms. What she couldn't see was why Yellow was rambling on about them. Perhaps the recent damage to the AI had been more extensive than it admitted.

'So? I don't see what they have to do with us and, presumably, a way of escaping this ship.'

'When not in use they are stored in various rooms throughout the ship. Their work clothing is stored there too, and one of those rooms is not far from where you are now.'

She still did not understand what Yellow was getting at or, at least, that's what she told herself. Deep inside she felt a lurch, and that began to surface in her mind as panic.

'This has no relevance!' she exclaimed.

'When the blanks move throughout this ship they are completely ignored, just like, before Penny Royal put you in that spider, you would have ignored a cleaning robot coming out of it hide in the base of a wall.'

She had to object again: 'This is irrelevant!'

'As I told you before,' Yellow continued relentlessly. 'I'm very good at sneaking around, but an eight ton mechanical spider, not so much.'

She wanted to object again, but knew she would not stop Yellow from taking this to its conclusion.

Yellow continued, 'Some good part of Penny Royal's mind put in you the ability to regrow your body, while a bad part made that predicated on you feeding on prador. And you damned well know that good Penny Royal also installed a separation routine.'

'The human body is dead,' she said.

'You don't know that but, if it is, then there is no escape for you, and you can blithely and happily allow the prador to disassemble you. Now, I'm going to take a look at those docking clamps. We'll talk later.'

The communication stopped with an almost audible click. Jenny just lay there fighting the surges of panic passing through her. Even so, like someone picking at a scab, her attention kept straying inward towards her soft core, but then retreating as that raised another surge of panic. It seemed, in the end, the only way to stop it was to forget what Yellow had been getting at and accept her fate here, on this column of exotic prador metal. However, two prador arrived, a chrome one and another with leaf green armour etched with a bright red Rorschach blot. They approached her front end, dropping heavy tool chests, which folded open to display glittering contents.

'You can understand me,' clattered the chrome one.

It was a distraction – a good timely distraction.

'I can also reply to you,' she said in the same clattering and bubbling prador language.

The prador moved over one of the tool chests and took up various tools and other implements. It then moved round to one side and climbed up on top of her. Her response was instinctive, and she extended her cantilevered chelicerae and partially extruded her fangs from them. She felt a surge of mild frustration. The prador was actually on top of her and she simply could not get to it. Her fangs, following the spider design, were only capable of stabbing down into something she was on. She extended them even further when the other prador moved in close in front of her, and now contemplated using her railgun. But the feeling, brought on by close proximity to the creatures, began to fade. She really didn't want to kill them and, now, felt just a passing ghost of the urge to feed.

'Well that's convenient,' said the green prador.

It shot forwards and snapped its claws closed on her chelicerae. The chrome one brought its claws down from above and got a grip too. Instinct rose again and she began to fight them. She discovered they were incredibly strong – stronger than any other prador she had faced. Was that because of more powerful armour or because of their underlying mutation? She began to test that strength, upping the power to the thread and stepper motors in her chelicerae and to the bearing meta-material surfaces. Soon she surmised that she could pull her chelicerae back in or perhaps give the prador ahead a thump, but to what purpose? Instead she just sat there wondering what they were going to do.

The chromed prador had its underhands ahead of her eyes. It reached down with an assortment of tools and some heavy metal items that looked to be of the same alloy as the column. It worked fast with all six of its hands and then brought in rods that arced, briefly blinding her. As her sight recovered she saw that both sections of her chelicerae had been manacled with connected rings of alloy and welded down to the column. She strained against that as the welding, after that pause, continued. At first she got a little movement, but as the weld extended that died away.

'Why are you doing this?' she asked. 'It's not as if I can ambush you.'

'The main reason is to get to this,' said the green prador.

It brought in another tool gripped in four of its hands, and started it up. It was a simple electric drill but, when she scanned it more deeply she noted supplemental vibration effects and that the drill bit itself consisted of exotic metal, shot through with pipes running chain diamond to its tip. Turning the tool to the required angle the prador began to drill down. It satisfied her to see how much trouble the prador had even getting a start. After a while whiffs of smoke began to rise and the tip of the drill began to glow. The prador triggered something and now a milky fluid flowed down the pipes in the drill bit, cooling it. Cutting increased and her armour came away as a black sludge. Now seeing that they would manage to penetrate through she scanned and built a 3D model of the drill in action on her to see where the hole would lead. It would go through the electrostatic barrel through which the rails of her railgun ran. She did not need to speculate much on the purpose of this.

'I can't really use this weapon against you,' she observed.

'At the moment, no,' the chrome one replied.

The drilling continued. Once through her outer armour its speed of penetration accelerated and she began routing around its damage. Just to be awkward she lined up an internal pipe carrying repair nanites, so she could rapidly fill in the hole when Chrome retracted the drill. Finally it broke through into her railgun and she ramped up the pressure to the pipe. It was petty, but relieved a growing ennui.

After breaking through green prador triggered something else on the tool. The drill bit detached from it and remained in place. The prador then attached a pipe to the back end of the drill bit. A second later another fluid came down the pipes and into her railgun barrel. Under pressure it filled the barrel in an instant and began to spill elsewhere so she hurriedly blocked it. The fluid heated with an abrupt chemical reaction, and solidified. Some kind of resin she could analyse, but she doubted the prador had introduced a chemical key for this stuff. Most likely she would need to clean it out piece by piece and it doubtless had defences against that. Her railgun was now out of action, and hadn't been much use to her anyway. Finishing their task at her front end, the chrome one clambered off. The two prador put away their tools and closed up their boxes.

'I still can't see why you did that,' she said.

'Just following orders,' the chrome one replied, and the two prador departed.

She thought about what they had done for a little while. Of course, they wanted her as intact as possible and knew that if she used the railgun the blowback would damage a lot inside her. This led on to thoughts about how else she could damage herself. She soon saw there were plenty of ways. She could detonate her missiles within, run power where it wasn't supposed to go burning out much of her system. She could, if she wanted, commit suicide. The prospect arose for her inspection and she dismissed it. But still remaining, after what they had done, was an intensification of the feeling of powerlessness. Now she did not like it at all and, with a feeling of heavy inevitability, turned her attention inward against a steadily waning panic.

She started out at her periphery and worked her way in. Her abdomen and cephalothorax had been welded down to the column, but this did not interfere with the . . . separation routine.

It has always been there open to her inspection and ignored or otherwise avoided as what it separated *from*. The line of division in her armour ran down either side of her cephalothorax. It wasn't straight but castellated on the outside and with castellation on the inner layers of armour not lining up, so that no strength would be lost. Once she gave the signal, meta-material layers would separate, and at the last the whole upper section of the cephalothorax would hinge up from the abdomen. She noted in passing that this was a bit like how prador got out of their armour. However, there were many more complications. The technology within was dense tech and packed in around the container holding her human form. It also penetrated that form but, still reluctant to look there, she concentrated on the surrounding tech.

Superconducting power threads, optics, nanotubes, microtubes, data ribbons and even larger tubes wove together a great mass of 'black box' components of her system. She had data processing in there, layers of laminar power storage, fusion nodes, discrete factories to make nanomachines, nutrient processors running to those other organic non-human parts of her and more besides. All of this, initially, had been provided with ways so that the lower half could disconnect from the upper half, which would rise attached to the cephalothorax lid. But now she began to see that many of these were missing. Years of damage and repair had altered her internally and, doubtless designed by bad Penny Royal, they had erased many of the plugs and sockets, valved pipe connectors and data shunts. She felt almost glad of that. Maybe she simply could not leave this spider body. Maybe that was best.

Her thoughts returned to what the prador had tried to prevent: her damaging herself, her committing suicide. She could switch down containment on her fusion nodes and ramp up power production. At some point the latter would overrun the former and create a hundred and twelve small suns inside her. She could link that to her munitions stores – feeding the overload straight into them. The result, for the prador, at best would be a burned out husk. Two options. She could set herself up for destruction or restoring what was missing in the separation routine. Tentatively, more as an intellectual exercise and something to keep her occupied, she began working on both options. It was just another form of procrastination.

'That's the clamps severed,' Yellow suddenly interjected, 'and now I'm inside the picket and in its system. How are things with you?'

'You don't know?'

'I told you I'm not connected to your mind, though I did see them come in and disable your railgun.'

'They don't want me damaging myself. Which is oddly amusing since they cut my legs off.'

'Most of the good stuff is in the spider body,' Yellow said. 'The repair nano-systems and manufactories. Good stuff in the legs too, but not so much.'

'I am looking at the separation routine,' said Jenny. She felt almost guilty about not telling Yellow that she was also looking at how to destroy herself.

'But still you haven't looked at *you*, I would bet.'

'True.'

'Y'know,' said Yellow. 'I think I can take this picket away from the ship without them even knowing it's been stolen. One of the other ones left just an hour ago to fetch supplies – their routines for that don't go all the way up to the captain.'

'Oh really,' said Jenny, noting the abrupt swerve away from the subject in hand.

'The prador are really quite wasteful and their ships need frequent resupply. They don't have the recycling efficiency of Polity ships, but then I guess the prador don't have that history of predictions of planetary disaster and existential panic the human race had.'

'Existential panic?'

'A period in human history when humans started to get too comfortable and, trying to avoid the realisation that they are just biological machines for passing on genes, started finding problems in their environment that didn't exist.'

'This is hardly relevant to our situation.'

'Just making conversation,' said Yellow. 'Speak to you later.'

And the AI was gone again.

Jenny felt suddenly annoyed and, almost in a fit of pique, focused all her attention, abruptly and without limitation, on her soft core. And there she lay, facedown with her arms stretched out, crucified on technology inside the spider. She wasn't skinless anymore and even had a buzz of blond hair on her skull, albeit around the numerous interface plugs there. She inspected these, remembering a spider in her skull, and wondered if that had been an amusing hallucination Penny Royal had introduced because scanning inside she could see no sign of it. She inspected all this closely. Her skull was full of nano-threads and neural meshes leading to those interface plugs. She could see that they would easily detach, leaving circular flat sockets which, to a passing prador, might even look like leech scars. More of these were distributed down her body and would be no problem. Of more concern were the connections into her digestive system and other major organs. These ran to the semi-organics of the spider body where she processed the juice sucked out of prador. Tracking things round she then noted how most of this could be disconnected. In fact, all the connections seemed a pointless complication, since all the juice went into the spider digestive system, which weaned out the organics required for itself and fed back only a little human digestible organics to the tube going in through her mouth into her gut. Ports to the veins in her chest, she noted, ran her blood through a meta-material gills. She wasn't breathing, but now, as she closely studied herself, something thumped.

Jenny retreated in panic, scanning around for danger. The room was empty, but then the thump came again, then again, stuttering occasionally before settling down into a steady rhythm. She started running diagnostics, first getting a lengthy list concerning her lack of legs, and then status updates on internal repairs and the nanites struggling to remove the resin filling her railgun, but beyond these nothing was really wrong. Realisation arrived with one of those thumps, and she returned her attention to her body. She thought then of Schrodinger and how the act of observation changes the observed. It seemed this cat was alive.

Her heart had started beating. Panicking anew she just could not see how this had happened. Now she noticed other movement – all the muscles of the body twitching frenetically. Something then started gurgling within. Had she inadvertently triggered the separation routine? Surely that wasn't possible? She watched the body and began a close AI level inspection of what was happening. After a short while the muscle shivering ceased, and shortly after that the heart stopped beating. And then she found it: a regular routine to keep the musculature, including the heart, functional. However, because she had been looking when this happened she felt a dislocation, a dragging inward as her sense of self positioned back inside that body. It felt weird, uncomfortable and, almost in a fit of rebellion, she forced her perspective back out and inspected her preparations for self destruction. All of that was ready and easy to initiate – just a program she needed to load. This now seemed wrong, that one option should be ahead of the other.

Jenny returned to the separation routine. Many points of disconnection were being restored, but what did they matter? Them not being in place only meant that if she started the routine it would carry on through. The only disadvantage would be damage to the system of the spider body she had been contemplating destroying anyway. The two options rose and fell in her mind. Did she really want to kill herself? The best answer was that she didn't really care. And the separation routine? There was no guarantee she would survive it, or that she could survive getting from this room to the picket of which Yellow was taking control. She pondered on this and remembered the humans who suffered the ennui of great age – how they kind of wanted to die and didn't, how they pursued riskier and riskier activities. That seemed the key in her mind and, without a second thought, she started the separation routine.

Her human body started shivering and twitching again, and the heart restarted. The even thumping seemed to pull her down and in. She felt her insides gurgling as technology began to disconnect all around her, and with that her perception of that technology began to wane. She felt the pipe sliding out of her mouth, gagged and felt soreness of her throat. An even more unpleasant sensation began to arise she could not identify, until her chest heaved and she took a metallic breath, laced with putrefaction. A hand twitched and she could feel the softness of her fingers, while she saw the blood shunts detaching. Panic returned and she tried to run, but the very idea of moving six legs seemed to rip out of her mind, and two legs kicked in the compartment. It all seemed to be going too fast for her, as if she was ripe and ready to shed her long worn skin.

Having now made her choice she rushed to make the best of it. With a fading grip she began using internal mechanism to sever and separate all those parts of her system that did not have ready points of disconnection. With a crump she felt deep inside her soft body, which had now entirely become her centre, as it had once been long ago when there had been a great deal less of it, the outer armour of her cephalothorax separated. She worked frenziedly now, little caring about damage to the spider body, overriding safeties and using internal lasers to slice through pipes, ribbons, power storage surfaces. Even as she did this she became more and more human and, in her human body, she felt an interface plug detach from her skull and part of her overall perception die. Inner layers of armour now began to part, and then, the upper part of her cephalothorax began to rise. All at once with a crackle like lightning through her mind, all the interface plugs disconnected. And she was blind.

No, not blind...

She opened her sticky eyes to get a blurred impression of a gut-like metallic tangle. She could hear sounds of mechanical and liquid organic movement. She hated it. How could she accept the limitations of human perception? What she could see was mere reflection from internal lasers and that dying now. She could not see through what sat in front of her face. She could not see all the activity around her. And she could not see beyond her erstwhile body. Movement now, something tugging her back and up. As this occurred she gained greater perception of her body and minimal collection of limbs. How could she accept that too? Yet, even as she posed the question, she accepted. She took another breath, and then another, but the air gave her no oxygen. Then, with a loud crump, a cacophony of tearing and lethal sounding electrical shorts, she began to rise up. Air immediately came cleaner and she gasped at it, then abruptly started coughing, bringing up chunks of phlegm and spitting them out. It felt so strange to have such a small wet mouth now, and tongue, and teeth. Eyes filled with tears, and she blinked, clearing them, to take in the simple human binocular view of the chamber she was in and the door ahead. And she was once again Jenny Kelland.

A choice had been made and now she needed to pursue it to its conclusion. Her purpose was to get out of here. She felt stupid not questioning Yellow about this room where blank clothing was kept, or how to get to the picket. There might be a solution to that but first she needed to get out of her erstwhile eight ton mechanical spider body. Tipping her head forward she inspected herself. With her arms outspread she was in a kneeling position, her lower legs going back into the abdomen. She tested her right arm, found resistance and tugged against it, finally dragging the limb from sticky gel with a couple of tubes detaching from her forearm. Where they detached they left two composite disks that welled blood for a second from central holes before small irises closed those holes off. She recognised simple medical venous shunts. She pulled her other arm free and found the same, though the tubes did not detach. Reaching across with a hand that seemed painfully simple, she pulled them out and watched the irises close. Numerous wires and other tubes still trailed from her arms and she quickly stripped them away, feeling a stab of urgency. Surely the prador was watching, or had otherwise been alerted. She needed to move fast.

All down her body some of the tubes and wires had detached and some not. She quickly pulled them free, hesitating only briefly over large ones leading into her intestines but finding they came away as easily as the blood and lymph tubes. Finally her visible body was clear and she pulled a leg free and got it forward, most of the tubes and wires there detached by that action. Then she got the other leg out and carefully eased herself from the spider shell and over the edge of the column to the floor. Her legs gave way at once and she went straight down on her backside on rough gratings. Something rose up inside her, difficult to suppress and not recognised until it came out of her mouth: she laughed. That she had managed to get this far without collapsing was amazing and of course due to the technology of the *good* Penny Royal. It had allowed her to regrow her body and kept it toned with those routines. The mental disconnection was thorough too, because now she could hardly imagine moving about on six legs. She slowly stood up and inspected herself again. Here she was: a completely naked and vulnerable human female aboard a prador ship. The sense of that impelled her into motion again.

She walked back around the column, delighted to be able to walk, but then stumbling when she thought about the action. Obviously the mental disconnection was not as complete as she supposed. New unpleasant sensations now began to impinge and, so long unfamiliar with them, it took her a moment to identify them. She felt sore wherever any of the pipes and wires had connected to her body. She felt bruised, and her insides were gurgling with nauseating hunger. Everything she touched felt hard and dangerous, including the rough floor under her soft feet. But, able to get some perspective on all this, she decided that after a few centuries regrowing and lying in gel, she shouldn't grumble.

Reaching the rear quarter of the spider abdomen she inspected the pitted and scarred surface, and finally found the yellow coin-sized spot. Would it work? She reached out to dig at it with soft fingernails but couldn't shift it for a second, then it abruptly bubbled up and she could, peeling it off like a thick scab. She held it in the palm of her hand. An attempt at speech resulted in another fit of coughing and a sickening quantity of green blood-streaked phlegm, but then her vocal cords began responding.

'Can you hear me, Yellow?' she managed.

No response at first, but then a tinnitus whining followed by a flash in her vision. She saw a cartoonish image of a human head with a series of red spots all over it. One, however, just above the right ear was green. She reached up to feel the interface sockets in her skull protruding from the buzz of hair, found the one indicated and pressed Yellow's remote against it, where it stuck in place at once.

'Get the hell out of there!' said Yellow.

Jenny headed straight over to the door, but then just halted. The thing was one of those heavy diagonally divided doors prador favoured. A pit control to one side, made to take a prador claw, opened it. She stepped up to it then held out her hands and looked at them. She knew exactly how the door control operated – she had opened many of them – but did she have the strength in human hands? She reached in to where the edges of the claw mated in the outer ring, braced the heel of a hand up against one side and got her elbow pushing down on the other, took a breath and heaved. The door control turned so easily she lost balance and went down on her ass for a second time. With just a slight whine of stepper motors the door parted – its two halves turning into the walls. Back on her feet she stepped through quickly.

'Go right,' Yellow instructed.

She nodded, but turned back to the door and operated the control on this side, setting it closing again before moving off. The pit control had been easier than any she had operated while in spider form. She put that down to these reavers being more efficient and well built, or to the King's children having better technology, yet still it somehow bothered her.

The oval tunnel without appeared lined with stone slabs, but they were probably foamed composite. The fact that many of them emitted the ambient light here attested to them not being real stone. Gratings ran along the floor and along the ceiling. It struck her as likely they ran grav from either above or below, depending on requirements, or most likely not at all since prador were perfectly designed for moving about in zero gee. In passing she thought they probably operated grav just to clean this tunnel and drop accumulations of debris, of which prador produced a lot, through the gratings. As she walked, keeping her pace steady and metronomic just as she remembered that of human blanks she had seen, she saw other cleaners of prador debris. Ship lice crawled along the walls, some of them quite natural and some with cybernetic additions. Creatures that for centuries she all but ignored, now made her shudder. With every passing moment she became more aware of her soft human nakedness. One of those lice could easily take a chunk out of her, and here, in this ship, she could be ground up in the workings in an instant.

'Twenty metres ahead on your right,' Yellow informed her.

The human scale door, inset in a larger prador door, was easy enough to recognise. Coming to stand before it, she studied a palm lock. Usually, in the Polity, these were set to open to only the correct hands – reading palm prints and DNA. She tried it anyway and, with a thump and hiss the door swung inwards. She stepped in.

The large and circular space beyond had room enough for a prador to get in here for maintenance, or whatever. All around, sarcophagus shapes indented the walls. Three of these contained human blanks. They were naked, held in place by heavy metal clamps, their faces half-concealed by thick straps holding tubes in place in their mouths. She gave them only a glance and searched around for the mentioned clothing, finding the armoured overalls piled in the last of a series of upright cylinders at the back of the room, along with footwear. Sorting through these she found most of them badly damaged. She was holding one set when something thumped in the cylinder and all its contents disappeared with a gust of air and a sucking sound. She jumped back, suddenly scared now of discovery.

Another cylinder nearby, which had been empty, thumped a few times too. Stepping over she peered inside at large coin-like packages. Automatic system, she realised, as she took one out, stripped off a fibrous covering and found new overalls and footwear. She put the overalls on, noting the heavy padding and hard plates of composite armour in them. There was no provision for human comfort in either overalls or the heavy shoes, beyond that they were shaped to the human form. Now, thinking on all those damaged sets of overalls, she walked over to the three blanks and studied them more closely.

All three were heavily muscled, bald, covered in leech scars, and a deeper shade of blue than she had seen before. By their body shape she assumed the two on the right were male and the other a female – she had flared hips and the remains of one breast. Both the males lacked the usual genitalia – just the stubs perhaps of penises and no testicles. All three were badly injured . . . or damaged. One male looked like he had been all but cut in half at the waist and then roughly stapled back together. The arms of the female next to him ended just beyond the elbow, where new knotted up human hands and forearms were growing. The final female brought home to her their real nature, for part of her skull was missing to show the interior occupied by a cylindrical prador thrall, its insect legs braced against the interior of her skull to hold it in place. She turned away and headed back to the door. This sight, more than anything else, brought home her vulnerability here. These blanks were incredibly old, rugged, tough and practically immortal creatures, yet here were three of them that had been damaged in ways that would kill her, and probably just during their general duties.

'Turn right and just keep going,' said Yellow. 'You'll eventually come to a shaft leading down from your present perspective, but grav will be out.'

'What do I do if prador come?' she asked. 'They may see that I'm not one of their blanks. . .'

'Unless they see what's happened with your erstwhile spider body and are actively looking for you – they haven't yet – they won't notice any difference. They find it difficult to distinguish one human from another.'

'How do you know they haven't discovered my . . . escape?'

'I left a piece of myself on your old body – just enough to keep watch.'

She nodded at that, but the explanation seemed too pat.

Yellow continued. 'You'll notice along your route alcoves occasionally set in the walls of the tunnels, or pits over to one side. These are generally so second-children can get out of the way of first-children, but are also used by blanks. If you see prador coming, try to get to one of those, but don't run – try to alter your pace to get you there on time.'

She found herself walking past one even as Yellow finished its instruction. The hole was large and round, went a metre down into the floor at its nearest edge and deeper at the back since it intersected with the oval of the tunnel. It was the right size to accommodate the average second-child. In that respect it seemed superfluous, since these King's children were all a lot larger and, knowing their aversion to discovery, she doubted any of the normal kind of prador were aboard.

As Yellow had said, she came to a shaft leading nominally down. It sat at a junction with her tunnel spearing on ahead, others leading left and right and the shaft continuing above. As she approached she felt grav waning. The top of the shaft was funnel-like – the lip curving down. The disappearing grav screwed with her perspective in ways she now remembered, but which had not been present in her spider form. Her shoes had no gecko grip so in the end she had to squat down and edge forwards gripping the gratings. She doubted this was how the blanks here did it, but she still felt too vulnerable to just fling herself forwards. Halfway down the curve grav was all but non-existent. The shaft was oval like the tunnel behind – all but indistinguishable from it – and she towed herself down gripping the gratings on one side.

'Where to now?' she asked.

'Three levels down then a side tunnel there – with grav in it – running directly opposite to the section you're crawling down.' Yellow paused, then added, 'I'll point it out to you when you're there, since you may lose your sense of direction.'

That wasn't all she was losing. She abruptly halted her steady progress and clung to the gratings. Her head was spinning and the rising nausea was now instantly recognisable. She retched, spitting out more blood streaked phlegm, then abruptly threw up a great load of green bile immiscible with a grey metallic looking liquid. How she could throw up so much when her spider body hadn't fed for so long and she felt so hungry she had no idea. The stream of vomit shot down the shaft, hit the grating a few metres ahead of her, spattered that and otherwise spread out in glutinous globules that seemed to move almost as if alive.

'Seems the zero gee adaptation wasn't included in your new body,' said Yellow dryly.

'Seems that way,' she agreed.

Jenny gritted her teeth against the nausea, pushed off from this side of the shaft, drifted across and gripped the gratings on the other side. This was to avoid the vomit cloud and because the tunnel she would next turn into ran from this side. The nausea was just as strong and she felt awful as she worked her way down the shaft. Finally, with the promise of grav in the tunnel she was to turn into, she kicked off and flew down at speed. That was when she saw the prador coming up.

Stupid!

Thankfully she wasn't too far from the gratings and reached down to slow her progress. Soft fingers bashed against the metallic composite and she began to drift away before wildly grabbing and abruptly halting her progress. She pivoted round on that grip and her forehead slammed down. With lights flashing in her vision and more immediate concerns, her nausea disappeared. She focused on the creature coming from below, lazily kicking against the edges of the tunnel to send it upwards. Between her and it, lay one of those recesses. Could she get to it in time? Or was there one closer behind? Looking back she could not see one so steadily propelled herself forwards. Her vision began to get bad and she could feel something crawling on her forehead and face. Touching her fingers there they came away bloody. Thankfully, however, she reached that recess and pulled herself into it.

The clack clack of the prador feet against the tunnel drew closer and began to slow. Frightened as she had not been in centuries, she observed small spurts of blood issuing from her forehead and breaking into streams of droplets in the air. Reaching up she found a flap of skin from under which the blood was pulsing, put a hand against it and pressed down. The prador, again one of the large King's children, clad in silver-grey armour decorated with thin blue lines in quadrate patterns like a Greek key, drew opposite and halted. With a lazy flip of a claw it turned to face her. Through its visor she could see an array of green eyes that certainly weren't prador standard.

'Just don't move and don't speak,' Yellow instructed.

Gripping a rough lip of the recess she froze, with her hand in place on her forehead. Oddly, her earlier fear faded, despite there being more reason for it now. Yellow had told her that blanks were ignored, yet here was a prador paying attention to her. Despite the AI's instructions she knew that if this creature paid any more attention – if it for example reached out to her with one of those claws – she would throw herself from this recess and get away from it just as fast as she could. She wasn't a blank. Any physical interaction with a prador would likely leave her in bleeding chunks floating in this shaft.

The prador shifted, propelling itself a little closer, then halted, with one claw opening and closing as if it really wanted to reach out and snip her in half. Abruptly, crashing that same claw against the edge of the tunnel, it turned and shot away. She breathed out the tight breath she had been holding, then tentatively took her hand away from her head. The bleeding had stopped, so it seemed that a standard genetic human upgrade – that of fast wound healing – *had* been included in her new body. As she propelled herself out of the recess and on down the shaft, she noted her nausea wasn't returning. Perhaps that upgrade had taken a little while to kick in.

'That was too damned fucking close!' Yellow exclaimed.

'Yes, indeed,' she replied, wondering why Yellow's words seemed so false.

'I suspect it saw the blood and that made it curious,' the AI went on. 'Blanks do have blood but it has the consistency of jam.'

'It perhaps thought I had a larger injury, bringing out that jam blood, and just stopped to check,' she tried.

'Yes, that seems plausible,' Yellow eagerly agreed.

Something wasn't right, but she had yet to plumb it. Prador in general weren't stupid, and these King's children were scary smart. This one had seen her bleeding liquid blood and thereafter stopping to inspect her. It must have noticed the interfaces in her skull. Prador also had similar colour perception to humans, so surely it would have seen that her skin wasn't the usual drowned man shade with its scattering of royal blue rings?

She passed the first and second junction without event, turned into the third one without any direction from Yellow, and gratefully walked in grav again. Her thoughts now began to stray beyond her immediate circumstances. Say she did get aboard that picket and say they did manage to escape the prador realm, what then? These thoughts brought vague grey mental constructs of her own life prior to the prador, and then Penny Royal, changing its course. They seemed float in her mind like large complex puzzle pieces she could not fit anywhere. She thought about Gogh, who she had thought vaporised and spread across a few million miles of vacuum, and of his particular penchant. Why was she thinking about that now? She pushed it away and thought about other people she had known. With the technology around even when the *Shinkansen* was destroyed some of them would still be alive now, though some, she supposed, had died in the war. Did they really concern her? No, she remembered that she hadn't been much of a social creature. Family? Back then she had a brother and two sisters, parents, grandparents and one great grandfather, but during her time with Gogh she had grown increasingly distant from them – rare communications feeling like a duty rather than a need. No, a life beyond all this would have to be something new.

Lost in speculation, she hadn't been paying sufficient attention to her surroundings, as she crossed another junction. The prador at the head of the column – in chromed armour and possibly one of those she had seen before – simply batted her aside with one claw. She flew back, bounced along the floor, skidded and tumbled and ended up down on her face. Blood flowed from the newly opened scalp wound. Looking up she saw another of those recesses nearby and tried to crawl towards it on her hands and knees. She groaned in pain putting pressure down on one hand and noticed the odd angle of her hand to her arm. Broken. Standing she felt further stabbing pains in her torso. Ribs too, it seemed. She stumbled into the alcove and squatted, only now seeing the line of prador moving off down the cross tunnel. There were ten of them and, beside the chromed one, all sported Gatling cannons.

'You are hurt,' Yellow observed.

'No shit, Sherlock,' she said, dredging up a saying from her far past.

'Once these are past you need to move fast. They've seen your spider body open and are searching the ship.'

'Well how is it that these didn't grab me? Surely they're checking all their blanks?'

After a short pause Yellow replied, 'Maybe they are not part of the search, or maybe they don't even know what they're looking for yet.'

'Yes. It must be that,' she said sourly.

She thought about how she had been scanned in that spider body, how the prador knew what her soft core was. She thought about that cephalothorax standing open exposing the human-shaped compartment within. Yellow's explanation was precarious at best. But what could she do? Call the AI a liar and try to find her own way of escaping? No. She had a broken arm and broken ribs and her only salvation was to get to that picket. And, anyway, she felt she had some understanding of the reason for at least some of those lies. . .

'Move fast now. Don't worry about not being seen as a blank – I think we're way past that now,' said Yellow. 'Continue as you were going and take the second left you come to. If you see prador now . . . run away from them and try to find somewhere to hide. I'll direct you from wherever you end up.'

Driven urgency, but she went with it. Out of the recess and cradling her arm, she broke into a jog, but the pain in her chest increased and she had to slow. After a couple of paces the urge to cough arose and she fought against it, knowing how painful it would be. Then she did cough, bringing up phlegm again but this time with a lot more blood in it. The pain continued to nag and even after coughing her lungs gurgled as she breathed.

'Punctured lung, I think,' she said.

'Keep moving now,' said Yellow, sounding distracted.

She reached that second left and headed down it. The prador were searching for her and along her course she noted more ship lice of the cybernetic kind and thought about how one of the chromed prador had sent these in search of Yellow. It seemed ridiculous that she had got so far. Perhaps the prador were not all that anxious about finding her? What they wanted she had left behind, and they probably saw little danger in one soft human stumbling through their ship.

The tunnel was short and opened out onto a grated gangway. On the near side a wall curved up. On the other side of the gangway stood rows of machines and masses of pipework that stretched up and down disappearing into shadow. The sudden change in perspective made her feel dizzy and she stumbled. She coughed again, spattering blood down the front over her overall. Hot and feverish now she looked along the gangway in both directions.

'Way. . .' she managed.

'Left, turn left,' said Yellow, now sounding angry. 'No if you go –' The words cut off, and she had the distinct impression that Yellow had started to address someone else before realising the link was still open to her. The turned left and kept walking, painfully, and now finding the nausea returning even though this area was not zero gee. She retched painfully, bringing up more blood. Great – not just her lungs, then. Ahead she saw a wide pipe extending from amidst the pipes and machines on that right hand wall – its near end on the edge of the gangway. As she drew closer she could see a divided door covering that near end. Closer still and the two halves of that door thumped up away from the pipe and began to revolve apart. Dread settled inside her. She could not run, she could not hide and now felt so very very tired. Without even noticing the transition she found herself sitting on the gratings, leaning on one hand. Her weight on the arm seemed too much and she dropped carefully down, curled foetal on her side and watched the doors open fully. The prador, she knew, would not handle her gently. If they did not kill her immediately, just doing whatever they wanted to go with her next, just moving her in fact, would probably result in her death. She was bleeding internally and, judging by how fast she had lost strength, she was bleeding a lot. The door halves crunched fully open, out from the edges of the tube like iron wings. She watched and waited for prador, hoping to lose consciousness before they came, but what stepped out was not prador at all.

At first she thought a human blank had stepped out. The man was big and looked woody, fibrous – as if fashioned out of gnarled wood. As he turned towards her she realised he was naked and probably not human at all. He reminded her of how she had looked inside the spider before her skin had grown back: a Da Vinci anatomical drawing – in pencil and charcoal, for the bare muscles sketched in grey and white. However those muscles did not wholly cover his skeleton of chromed ceramal. He advanced quickly and stooped over too peer down at her. She could hear a slight whine of stepper motors, while his eyes, bare balls of amber, blinked irised shutters over them a few times, with clicks like an antique camera taking pictures. He stooped lower and carefully rearranged her, but even that elicited a groan of pain, and he scooped her up.

'Snickety snick,' he said. 'I got you right quick.'

The pain grew as he carried her towards that open door but, thankfully, her consciousness fled before it.

Some form of consciousness must have returned after the strange Golem carried her past those doors, because she felt deep puzzlement at the human scale corridors beyond it. She felt stoned, and very sick, but at least the pain had gone away. White surrounded her and it seemed far too bright, while a large and shadowy form stooped over her. Recognition of the surgical robot aboard Penny Royal's ship brought with it utter confusion. She saw bloody implements shifting down below her breasts and did not want to look too closely. Turning her head aside she found familiarity in a Polity operating room, and that only increased her confusion. Then the sight of another object in that room brought with it the prospect that her mind had snapped, or perhaps she was hallucinating.

The chainglass cylinder stood between the table she lay on and where a nanoscope and other standard Polity equipment littered a wall-mounted bench. The cylinder extended from a wide composite base inset with various controls, and from which pipes and skeins of wires strewed the floor. Similar pipes and wires webbed from the point where it met the ceiling. But it was what floated in the cylinder that challenged her sanity. Hooked up inside, like she had been when inside the amniotic tank aboard Penny Royal's ship, floated a human brain. This was odd in itself, but odder still was the body of a human foetus coiled below it. The brain, it seemed, had mushroomed from the weak neck, while concertinaed below it were vaguely recognisable human features.

'Lucky it didn't break her spine,' said a voice.

'Let's hope,' replied Yellow, 'that they don't think Mr Grey breached the agreement.'

'They were in breach – this should not have happened,' said the other.

The conversation continued, but thereafter made no sense. She drifted in that realm between sleep and waking where dream intersected reality and logic took a holiday. She heard the sound of bone and cell welders, and felt the surgical robot tugging at her torso. She had no sudden awakening; no sudden rise to full consciousness. At one point she found herself sitting upright, supported by the robot as it carefully wiped blood and other substances from her naked body. In the next clear point of consciousness the table had turned into a chair, while the surgical robot squatted over to one side, cleaning its implements like cat its paws. The feeling of acceleration trying to tip her out of the chair raised her to awareness. She grabbed one arm of it and realised she had done so with what had been her broken arm. The acceleration died. Lifting that arm to inspect it she could see no signs of the repair. Dropping her hand back into her lap, she found the pile of clothing there.

'We are away from the prador ship,' said Yellow.

Jenny looked around the room expecting to see the stain of the AI across one wall. She then reached up and felt her head. No sign of the split there – such a repair would have been child's play to a robot capable reassembling a human being. Probing higher she found the interface plugs still in place so doubtless a piece of Yellow remained there.

'So we have escaped?' she said.

'Yes, we've escaped!' Yellow exclaimed.

'Why are you continuing to lie?' she enquired.

After a long pause, Yellow said, 'This ship is an old attack ship, but of a design you would not have seen. If you turn left out of your present room and keep going, you'll reach the bridge.'

Jenny nodded and climbed out of the chair. She felt weak and shaky but far from incapable. She now went through the half-remembered process of putting on knickers and a bra, then tight black trousers, slippers and a white belted blouse. Only as the motion of her hands in this process brought a stab of nostalgic familiarity did she recognise the clothing as much the same as she had worn in another life.

At the door she palmed the lock to one side and stepped out. The corridor beyond was much larger than human scale and did have its hint of pradorishness. She saw why when a prador came towards her. He was smaller than the average second-child, utterly blue, and she could not tell whether he wore armour or she saw his natural carapace. Injuries remembered, she swiftly moved back against the wall feeling a stab of terror.

'Don't worry about Blue,' said Yellow. 'He's always very careful. He hadn't even made it into second-child status when the dreadnought he was aboard got trashed. Penny Royal found him floating in vacuum, still alive in his suit. Apparently he was utterly confused by how such weak creatures as humans destroyed his father's ship. Penny Royal enlightened him by meshing up his brain with one of the human survivors of that conflict. Impossible to separate them.'

The prador, its eye stalks watching her, moved to one side and carefully edge round, then headed off as if embarrassed by the encounter. She moved on and had got a hundred metres when she heard a buzzing behind her. The smiling head of a man, mounted on some saucer-like lump of technology floated past. He managed a nod, driven by shiny hydraulics attached to the back of his skull.

'Glad to have you with us,' he said. 'It'll be confusing at first, but you'll get used to it.' He floated on ahead of her, then disappeared down a side corridor.

Next an ophidapt woman stepped into sight. She had organic looking pulse rifles melded into each of her arms and a targeting hologram floating in front of her face. She said nothing – just marched past as if Jenny wasn't there. Jenny next passed under another prador, legless and stuck upside down to the ceiling, red eyes all around its head turret and around the edge of its main carapace too. Then a dwarf, seemingly fashioned of stone and who she had first taken to be a statue, abruptly turned from the wall and walked off. She halted and watched him go, vague knowledge hardening in her mind and taking a shape she had been evading for some time.

'Many here have been altered by Penny Royal,' she said.

'You're getting it,' Yellow replied.

'And how many of those here are those who survived, if that is the correct word, the prador attack on my ship?'

A long and heavy silence ensued.

'I don't remember much of that time,' the paint AI finally said. 'The stuff I told you about being a Golem artist is true, as with my sojourn in a flask in an ECS facility. When I worked for you I was on a journey of artistic discovery – abruptly terminated by the prador.'

'Do I call you Gogh?' she asked, and continued walking towards the bridge.

'It was just one of many names I had.'

'So Yellow Azimuth it is henceforth?'

'Yes, I would prefer that.'

Finally she reached a door that opened ahead of her, admitting her to the bridge.

Because the interior had been either screen painted or hung with screen fabric, she seemed to be walking out onto platform exposed to vacuum. A captain's chair at the centre sat empty as did other control stations running around the wall. Directly ahead, diminished by distance, the reaver hung out there. Stars of every hue of the rainbow dotted space, but no larger stellar objects were visible nearby.

'So where are you . . . Yellow?' she asked.

'All around you – I'm paint so here I function as screen paint.' Yellow paused for a second, then continued, 'No need really, but I like to keep busy.'

Jenny grimaced at the babbling, rounded the captain's chair and slumped down in it. It gave her an odd surge of nostalgia. She scanned around, feeling something twitch throughout her being, then almost burst out laughing at the ridiculousness of her looking for a small conglomeration of web-bound rubbish that would be the home of a trapdoor spider. She felt no fear; it was just a shadow of an ancient one.

'What happened?' she abruptly asked. 'Why have you been lying to me beyond concealing your identity? And by the way, why the hell did you do that?'

'Revealing who I *was* would have complicated the issue. You might have asked me about the time we spent together. I told you I can hardly remember any of it and, if I'd answered wrong you would have thought me a liar. Paranoia was a large part of your nature.'

'Okay, I'll accept that,' she said, though she didn't like it. 'But that wasn't the only lie you've told. . .'

'So what other lies concern you?' Yellow asked, amused.

'The prador could have stopped me. They let me go. There is no way I could have simply walked out like that. . .' This at least she was firm about, but when she searched inside herself to identify what seemed so wrong about all this, the logic of it just started to break up. She grasped those things she did know. 'This is no prador picket . . . and the others here. And that surgical robot. . .'

The screen paint rippled and, though Yellow was not something with an expression she could read, it seemed like laughter.

'We are the Survivors Club,' he said. 'As you have understood, those aboard this ship were, or are, beings transformed by Penny Royal. We only learned about you when, after learning about her, we took the surgeon from a Graveyard criminal organisation. Gillian is now, as you have seen, growing a new body.'

'Okay. . .' For a moment Jenny did not know what else to say, but then found the words. 'But the behaviour of the prador and you here now in this ship. There was no escape – this was all planned.'

'I have some memories that are clear,' said Yellow. 'I remember moving at speed down the length of our ship only to be incinerated as I reached the bridge, just outside the door. I remember black knives in the air cutting my crystal from the remains of my body. Could it have been that others nearby were retrieved? The thought gnawed at me for ages. . .'

'That's no answer,' said Jenny stubbornly, but could think of nothing to add, remembering that her concern at that moment had been killing a damned spider.

Yellow, or Gogh continued, 'It was one of the first things I asked Gillian, whose memory is extensive of the operations Penny Royal had her perform. Yes, Penny Royal took you too and she detailed everything that had been done to you. We modelled you and understood that just going to you and rescuing you from the planet would only result in us ending up with a huge spider drone that needed to feed on prador.'

Just then the doors behind opened and Mr Grey walked in. He rounded the captain's chair, looming over Jenny and peered down at her. He blinked his strange eyes, then abruptly turned away and went to sit in another chair, staring at the console before him.

'Don't mind him,' said Yellow. 'No one needs to be here since we can control this ship from wherever we are, but he likes to be at his weapons console when it seems likely he'll need to blow something up.'

'What?'

Mr Grey abruptly turned his chair to face in. He held up two fingers and scissored them. 'Snip snip,' he said.

'Weapons?' Jenny asked.

'We will get to that,' said a musical female voice.

Now another shape came into view from behind, moving with eerie silence on numerous legs. The surgeon settled down over to one side of the chair – now a telefactor from that strange foetus elsewhere in the ship.

'Yellow was giving you an explanation,' said Gillian. 'You need to hear it.'

A sigh emitted from all around, from Yellow, and the paint AI continued, 'You were the product of a fractured mind, Jenny. Good Penny Royal had made it so that once your human body had regrown you would lose your appetite and could abandon the spider body. Bad Penny Royal made it so that once your human body achieved a certain growth, it could never complete. At that point, every time you fed, your spider body converted substance of that human body into the digestive fluids you injected. Over the years in your network of burrows you kept reaching a point where you looked like Mr Grey here, then waned away to what you were aboard Penny Royal's ship.'

'Penny Royal was a bit of a bastard,' Jenny said.

'Penny Royal was God and the Devil rolled into one – if you know your mythology.'

'So then what happened?'

'I did.'

'What?'

'If I may,' said Gillian, holding up one glittering limb.

'Do continue,' said Yellow.

'We knew your location and using concealment as best we could we got this ship as close as we could,' she said. 'We learned that the prador thought you destroyed, but I surmised it unlikely a neutron blast could completely destroy you. But it was all just too risky that near the border. However, Yellow was insistent. He hitched rides on prador vessels to get to your world. Searched those caverns for five years before finding you in a water filled cavern, then introduced a fix I made, and you woke up.'

'The fix?'

'It started converting organics inside you to rebuild your body.'

'I see. . .'

'But of course that wasn't really enough,' Yellow continued. 'You had spent so long in spider form you needed time for your inner human to reassert. Once you revealed yourself and destroyed those drones, time ran out. The King, hearing of you and assuming you a Polity drone, sent his children to either capture or destroy you, so my compatriots revealed themselves and proposed a deal.'

'Deal?' Jenny prompted.

Yellow sighed. 'A deal that we may well have screwed. Listen and learn.'

A frame opened up in the screen paint – in the body of Yellow the paint AI. It showed the prador captain squatting in his sanctum. Unexpectedly he was surrounded by fish tanks swarming with life. Jenny was sure she could see some terran tropical fish there, but also alien creatures she could not identify.

'So you have her now,' said Vottle.

'We do indeed,' Yellow replied.

'Then return her to us and you can leave.'

'That wasn't our deal.'

'You defaulted.'

'And so did you.'

'I'm failing to see how.'

Yellow made a sound like a snarl through a rubber sheet. 'Our deal was that I would enable you to capture her, but in return you must help drive her psychology so she would abandon her spider body and come to us. You were not to harm her. And now you have that spider body with its load of Penny Royal technology.'

'And besides yourself – and you were to leave the ship as soon as feasible depositing only a method of contact – none of you Penny Royal creatures were to leave your vessel. I clearly remember all the details.'

'You were to allow her to escape without injury. You injured her.'

'An accident,' said Vottle, waving a dismissive claw.

'We have been round and round on this repeatedly,' said Yellow. 'It seems to me you are stalling, and have been for a while. Those other reavers closing in on this position have not escaped our notice, you know.'

'We have, as you say, a large piece of Penny Royal tech, but we could learn so much more by examining her and the technology installed in her body to interface with her erstwhile body.'

'Open U-com to your king. I think this is above your pay grade.'

'We will only need to examine her for a while. We will return her too you.'

'Undamaged?'

'Of course.'

'Liar. I rather suspect some overreach here. How high will you rise in your king's regard if you were to capture more than just one piece of Penny Royal tech?'

'You are cynical.'

'I am indeed, which is why I did this.'

Vottle abruptly spun round and moved out of view. After a short pause he came back and just stared out of the screen frame, saying nothing. Noticing something, Jenny looked to the main view of the reaver, and there saw a plume of flame issue from a port.

'That was just one of your chemical munitions. I imagine one of the CTDs will do a lot more damage. I also imagine, since they are on the other side of your ship from us, we'll be able to fly clear of the wreckage.

'You have now completely destroyed the deal.'

'Oh the parts of me scattered throughout your ship can do so much more. Especially those parts of myself inside that spider body. Perhaps a better option would be for me to destroy that, and watch while you explain the loss to your king?'

'I don't think –' Vottle began, but then the screen frame blanked.

'Now we're getting somewhere,' said Yellow.

When the frame came back on it showed some deeply, aseptically white interior. Into view now walked a nightmare. It looked like a huge louse – not the trilobite form of ship lice but a terran louse, with langoustine claws and long legs supporting it high off the floor. Scale was difficult to fathom until she saw the technology attached and in some cases penetrating the creature's body. She recognised some Polity hardware there and realised this thing must be huge.

'King Oberon,' said Yellow.

'Big big snip,' said Mr Grey

Jenny glanced over at the Golem. Mr Grey clicked his eye shutters at her and it seemed he was smiling, though with a face like his it was difficult to tell.

'It was worth trying,' said the King in a smooth androgynous Anglic.

'Your idea?' asked Yellow.

'No, Vottle's. I think our negotiations are complete now. I would allow you to leave, but I am not sure our acquisition will survive your departure.'

'It will survive,' said Yellow. 'Those parts of me will deactivate when we are past the border. Of course, if we are knocked out of U-space at the border, the disruption will not prevent me sending a signal. '

'And I am supposed to believe you?'

'There are still many others of our kind we have not yet found – Penny Royal was not anything but profligate with its gifts. Some will be in the Kingdom. I will not renege on this deal, since we may have further deals to make.'

The King waved a claw and the screen frame blanked again for a second before bringing back Vottle.

'You may leave,' said the prador.

How deep into her mind had Yellow ventured, Jenny wondered as she surveyed her cabin. It was the replica of the one she'd had aboard the *Shinkansen*, even down to the clothing hanging in the cupboard. Or perhaps his memories of the ship were more extensive and detailed than he seemed to indicate.

She went and sat down on the double bed, closed her eyes and listened to the slight hum of the ship around her, recognising the feel of flight through U-space. The prador might still yet operate a USER at the border to knock them back out into the real and seize this ship, and all the Penny Royal technology aboard. Yellow said otherwise. The King had a great deal of respect and fear of that technology. He might relish the prospect of getting his claws on more of it, but would know that his chances of capturing it intact, or not have it end up seizing control of those ordered to grab it, were remote.

So what now?

She had lived a human life time and the lifetime of a predatory beast in an underworld of her own making. Now she was back in human form and she did not know what to do – there seemed something undone, something incomplete. Her mind seemingly sliding through the cabin and out into her old ship she remembered all her struggles and their bright termination in the prador attack, and the ridiculousness of her spider concerns. But all of that carried no more emotional weight than memories of an entertainment created by someone else. She peered down in the corner of the room where she had once seen the trapdoor spider nest, and now memory took her into her system of burrows and her spider body. This, in its endless cyclic horror, had more immediacy and pulled up an awful feeling from her core. Her eyes closed, squeezing out tears and a fist closed up in her insides. She didn't know yet whether to cry or laugh hysterically at the feeling of loss for that life and not the one before. It seemed her restoration was far from complete and now as the storm rose up through her, she recognised this unfinished business. Just like Penny Royal, grief could not be negotiated with or circumvented, just survived.

ENDS

Printed in Great Britain
by Amazon